PHENOTYPES

Phenotypes

PAULO SCOTT

translated by Daniel Hahn

SHEFFIELD – LONDON – NEW YORK

This edition published in 2022 by And Other Stories
Sheffield – London – New York
www.andotherstories.org

Originally published in Portuguese by Alfaguara as *Marrom e Amarelo* in 2019

1 3 5 7 9 10 8 6 4 2

ISBN: 9781913505189
eBook ISBN: 9781913505196

Editor: Jeremy M. Davies; Copy-editor: Fraser Crichton; Proofreader:
Sarah Terry; Cover Design: Tom Etherington. Typeset in Albertan Pro
and Linotype Syntax by Tetragon, London. Printed and bound on acid-
free, age-resistant Munken Premium by CPI Limited, Croydon, UK.

And Other Stories gratefully acknowledge that our work is
supported using public funding by Arts Council England.

This book has been selected to receive financial assistance from English PEN's
PEN Translates programme, supported by Arts Council England. English
PEN exists to promote literature and our understanding of it, to uphold
writers' freedoms around the world, to campaign against the persecution and
imprisonment of writers for stating their views, and to promote the friendly
co-operation of writers and the free exchange of ideas. www.englishpen.org

Obra publicada com o apoio do Ministério da Cultura do Brasil /
Fundação Biblioteca Nacional. This work was published with the support
of the Brazilian Ministry of Culture / National Library Foundation.

Supported using public funding by
**ARTS COUNCIL
ENGLAND**

MINISTÉRIO DA CULTURA
Fundação BIBLIOTECA NACIONAL

CONTENTS

For my father

The official came up, opened the door without pausing to ask permission, stepped inside and gestured for me to join him. I stood in front of eight unfamiliar people waiting for me, those eight who made up the commission devised by the new government to find an adequate solution, just the latest in the new government's long list of mistaken adequate solutions, to the chaos that had resulted, suddenly, from implementing a policy of racial quotas for students in Brazil, that sleepwalking country, the giant ex-colony of the Portuguese crown in South America, branded across the world as a place of ethnic harmony, of oh so very successful miscegenation, a place where the practice of white men raping black and indigenous women had been allowed to run wild for centuries, and, as in almost all those lands christened the New World, had been assimilated, mitigated, forgotten, a place where, in the twentieth century, nobody ever dared, let alone seriously, to propose a law forbidding a black from getting together with a white, white with indigenous, indigenous with black, a country that's number one in the rankings of the planet's so-called racial democracies, an emblem of a kind of friendliness that is unique, indecipherable, and which people who don't know any better tend to generalise as being a sign of the unrivalled warmth of Brazil. Without waiting for me or one of the eight to speak, the official just started right in on introducing me, making a mistake straight off the bat, the same mistake so many other inattentive people make, with my first name, calling me *Frederico* rather than Federico, despite the fact that he was actually looking at an A4 page printed in fourteen-point Arial with a short CV, giving my correct name, a CV that he, disregarding the existence of that old thing called Wikipedia, could only have assembled from announcements he'd picked out of a totally indiscriminate online search. He reported that I had been one of the founders of the Global Social Forum in Porto Alegre, that I was an important researcher into the so-called hierarchy of skin colours, on pigmentocracy and its logic in Brazil, on the perversity of colourism, on compensatory policies and their lack of understanding among the Brazilian élites, that I'd advised NGOs in Brazil, in Latin America and the rest of the world, that I'd consulted for Adidas, oh yes that's right, Adidas, the famous German-founded company making high-performance sportswear, the man was foolish enough to emphasise, as if that were the high point of my biography, and I did consider interrupting him, saying like hell did I ever consult for Adidas, that I'd merely acted as intermediary for an agency that did advertising for them with some graffiti artists from the streets of Brasília for this series of videos they were making to stream on Vimeo, on YouTube, on Instagram, an action inspired by an old campaign produced in the US in the nineteen eighties around the slogan skateboarding is not a crime, but I ended up biting my tongue, I let him continue in the interests of keeping my blood pressure down as a forty-nine-year-old man already taking five milligrams of Naprix every morning to keep it under control, and the last person to be nominated by our distinguished new President of the Republic to be a part of this group of supposed worthies, and then, only then, when he reached the end, and not till he had given me a little good luck pat on the back, did he, the official who had got my name wrong, withdraw.

I sat down in the nearest chair knowing that the eight were waiting for something from me that might justify my arrival in the closing minutes of their first meeting. In my head, however, what predominated was the discomfort caused by the distance between my chair and theirs, the eight clumped together at the opposite end of the gigantic oval table, and also the contrast between my XXL skateboard freestyle T-shirt that sported the face of Ice Blue, the rapper from the Racionais MCs, Brazil's best rap group ever, printed really big on the chest, my Drop Dead trousers in orange with navy-blue thread and my Rainha VL Paulista sneakers in black with grey that were totally wrecked, which was in no way accidental, and their clothes, not to mention my canine distrust towards them, the flashbacks that were surfacing now and getting all jumbled up in my head, like the talk my mother had with me and my brother Lourenço when I was seven and he was six to try to lessen his confusion at the insults that had come out of the filthy mouths of three of his little bastard classmates from pre-school, classmates who, as early as the second day of school, called him Golliwog, Sambo, Magilla Gorilla, because in a game of tag during recess he hadn't submitted to their commands the way a Brazilian child who was

11

considered black, according to the imaginary common law of those Brazilian children considered white in that year of nineteen seventy-three, was supposed to submit. Those sermons of my mother's became commonplace in that same year of seventy-three, because I, wanting to defy her, wanting to make her responsible for this difference that hadn't previously existed with any particular aggressiveness in my life and my brother's, a difference that came to be reiterated through the mouths not only of a trio of irrelevant little pre-school demons but the mouths of older pupils, of some employees and possibly even the occasional careless teacher, about how we weren't brothers really, not blood brothers, saying things about one of us being adopted, despite both him and me replying, in that way children do, withholding nothing, that yes we were, we were real brothers, never mind that by the standards of those who were asking, by the standards of Porto Alegre, by the standards of that Brazil of that year nineteen seventy-three, I, with my very fair skin and straight brown hair verging on the blond, was considered white, and he, my brother, with dark skin, dark brown curly hair verging on the black, albeit with the same hooked nose, kind of wide, as mine and the same mouth with a thinner upper lip and thicker lower lip like mine, was considered black, insisting on asking my mother what race we really were, ignoring her responses about how colours and races didn't matter, that deep in our bones we were all the same, paying no mind to her assurances or to the fact that on the birth certificates drawn up at the Zone 2 Notary Office of the Porto Alegre Civil Registry of Births, Marriages and Deaths, according to the notary criteria implemented in the decade of the nineteen-sixties in the far south of Brazil, both he and I were registered as being mixed, while for her part, my mother, who knows, perhaps she was acknowledging all the while to herself that this business of one son being subjected to a kind of violence that the other son would never experience was a real piece of bad luck, just a seriously shitty quirk of fate, but of course speaking aloud the same words that would be repeated many times not only in the year seventy-three, but throughout my childhood, that we were all black, that she with her light skin and straight brown hair and my father with his dark if less dark than my brother's skin and really curly black hair, and then my brother and I as well, that our family was a black family, even at my eighth birthday, when my aunt, my mother's sister, showed up with her two kids, both considered white by the standards of nineteen seventy-four, not to mention the decades that followed, and with a cousin of theirs too, a proper little menace, oh so proud of his whiteness at that party of dark people, a kid my age, who, at a certain noisy interval in the process of children bonding at a birthday party, selected me as his adversary and started going on about how, in spite of my having hair that could be plastered down and lightened by the sun, my father's hair was still all fuzzy, all frizzy, and it was only good for cleaning the mud off the sole of his own father's shoe, his father who was white and had proper straight blond hair, and on account of which I watched for the conclusion of the series of games at that stage in the process of children bonding at a birthday party, when everyone was tired, bored or distracted, waiting for the moment when he, the menace, would let his guard down and move away from the area that was subject to adult observation and rescue, to approach him and, just like in all the thrillers I've ever watched on the three channels Brazil had in those days, bring my hands to his neck, push him against the wall and start choking him, growling I'm gonna kill you, then my dad's gonna kill your dad, and only failing to carry the strangling through to more serious consequences because my two cousins, a few years older than me, if physically far less substantial, grabbed my arms, forcing me to abandon the only reaction that had seemed appropriate to me, that is, to finish that kid off once and for all, to finish off any white who talked shit about my father, and then that start of a long weekend with my father getting ready to leave the house for the Ararigboia Park football pitch where he was going to compete in a four-way contest between the civil police team and the military police team, and my mother asking him to take me along, and him saying there was no way because it was going to be a pretty tense competition, since any interactions between the two police forces were usually pretty tense, and besides there wouldn't be anyone there who could look after me, and her saying she was sure he'd figure something out, and him getting annoyed but ending up surrendering to her request, and then, at the Ararigboia, him, my father, hearing that his team's coach wasn't going to show up because he'd had an attack of kidney stones and he was home on medication, meaning that the only person with enough good sense to take the coach's position, which according to the rules couldn't be left vacant, was my father himself, which meant in turn that he had to leave me with four guys who were already wearing the team kit while he went off to deal with the practical nuts and bolts of the substitution, replacing the name of the coach who hadn't shown up and writing in the new guy who would be playing in my father's place on the sign-up forms and on the squad list, and then the tallest of the guys wearing the team strip, a balding white guy, the moment my dad moved away to the other side of the pitch, asking hey is this kid really Ênio's boy, and one of the other three answering well he looks like Ênio, the final two keeping quiet, and the tallest balding white one insisting but he's too white, and a fifth guy dressed up in the same kit appearing behind me and immediately saying to the others so we got a new recruit on the team have we, and then, without giving me time to react, asking what's your name kid, and me answering that it was Federico, trying to look at his face but finding it hard because he was standing with the sun right behind him, and the tall balding white guy saying I was Ênio's son, and the new arrival saying whoah, that's cool, a big strong kid, just like his dad, and running his weighty hand over my head saying whoah, Federico, you look like someone who's gonna be a centre-forward-crushing defender, look how thick this kid's legs are, fellas, my money's on him, then heading off in the same direction as my dad, and me turning my attention back to the tall balding white guy, and the tall balding white guy with a dead-fish smile just looking at the other three while he scratched his chin and, at frantic micro-intervals, looking at me too, and what about that day in that week when there was no water for five days in Porto Alegre's eastern zone, including our street, and my father was taking us, for the third night in a row, to one of the buildings where he worked as a civil police forensics expert, where we'd fill up two large containers with drinking water and have a shower, and it was late at night, and my brother and I were excited, an excitement that came from the fact that it was the fourth day running we didn't have water back home, from it being late, about 11 p.m., but also from this argument we were having, the sort of pointless argument we were always getting into in those days of being brothers in their confrontation phase, an argument that started with an I'm having my bath first, which was answered with a no way you're so not, you had yours first yesterday and the day before yesterday too, today it's me going first, an argument that stretched out and which by the time my father emerged from the bathroom had already turned into shoves and insults, me attacking my brother with go fuck yourself, stupid little black dumbass, and him counterattacking with go shove it up your fag ass, desperate whitey wannabe, my father used to use that word wannabe when he wanted to refer to blacks with lighter skin who straightened their hair and were terrified of being taken for mulatto or of being recognised as black by someone who wasn't black, and this ended up being enough for him to put down his wet towel, grab us by the collars of our T-shirts and drag us to the training and weights room of that civil police building, a mini-gym where in addition to the workout equipment there was a padded-floor ring for judo and boxing matches, for him to turn on the lights, make us climb into the ring, pick up a skipping rope saying that if we wanted to fight then he'd make us fight, tossing two pairs of gloves at our feet, telling us to put them on, telling us if we didn't fight and while we fought didn't keep on insulting one another he was going to wallop us with that rope, me looking at him saying sorry, him telling me not to say sorry to him, saying that I, being the oldest, was the one who had to set an example, telling us to just put the damn gloves on already and hug, taking the rope and tying us up tight saying we'd be staying there stuck to one another to think about what it was that made one brother belittle another brother like we were doing, turning out the lights of the mini-gym and leaving, locking the door, returning twenty minutes later to find us untied, lying on the floor of the ring, next to each other, or the Wednesday morning when a guy from my eighth-grade class, a shy sort of guy and a good student I actually got on with kind of well, without anybody noticing, put two bananas into the rucksack of a classmate in the break between lessons and she, one of the few black students in that school, when she came back to the classroom with two other classmates, realising her rucksack wasn't in the position or the place where she'd left it, opened the zip and found the brown paper bag with the fruit inside, a paper bag on which somebody had written in magic marker Zoo Express, and one of the girls who was with her screamed oh, Jesus Christ, and went on repeating zoo, bananas, how horrible, so cruel, so disrespectful, ensuring there was no way the situation could possibly pass unnoticed by the rest of the class, a guy who ended up being exposed because he was on the school basketball team and I was also on the school basketball team, and the day after the banana incident, before practice started, when I went into the locker room to change into my kit, I caught him boasting to two other students, two of the ones who were on the handball team, which practised right before us, definitely the two most disturbed kids on the handball team, which was definitely the most disturbed of all the sports teams in the school, and when one of them asked whether she stank a lot or a little, that was when they noticed me, realising I was there doing nothing except listening to them, and me not bothering about them, and going off to practice like nothing had happened, but the next day, totally cool all of a sudden, walking over to the deputy principal's office and reporting him, which led to his being suspended from school and then my summary exclusion from the circle of basketball team jocks by most of the other guys on the team, guys who started calling me traitor or snitch and freezing me out in every way until, two months later, I, who was basically the toughest bastard in the whole fucking jock hierarchy on the school basketball team anyway, quit going to practice, quit basketball entirely, and then one Saturday in October nineteen eighty-two I lied to my parents and to Bárbara, with whom I was starting to develop the kind of relationship that meant she could perhaps be characterised as my high-school girlfriend, claiming that I was getting a lift with two other school friends to the family house of one of them up in the city of Gramado and that I was going to be coming back on Sunday night, when really what I did was take a bus on my own up to Caxias do Sul for the Cio da Terra festival, an event that was taking place in the pavilions of the Grape Festival Event Park and which had been promoted by the organisers as the first open gathering of the local 'gaúcho' youth, a festival of arts and talk where there would be no censorship, there would be no sexual repression, there would be no police, there would be no military types carrying rifles and being a pain in the ass, and there I got together with some guys I met at the bus station to split a few big bottles of wine, a few German kuchen, a piece of Colony cheese and a few whole pork salamis, sating my thirst, my hunger, and then I split off from them and wandered among the groups of people scattered around the park, listening to the shows from a distance, observing, trying to learn what it was that those hippies who were all older than me knew and I hadn't figured out yet, and it was only when it was time for Ednardo's set, round about three in the morning, that I decided to go over and watch, standing about fifty metres from the stage, captivated by his lyrics, until, when the performance was nearly over, a white man aged about fifty, in a kind of trance, walked past me saying, on a loop, I'm not seeing all the black youth here, and me, negotiating with the sobriety which in that year was the norm for my life, pretty dull aside from the chaos introduced by Bárbara's insanities, trailing after him, keeping my distance, also saying I'm not seeing all the black youth here, going around and reproducing his words, even after he, realising there was some total pain of a kid following in his footsteps, had given up on his trance, his walking around and his words.

Some of them looked straight at me, others looked at the screens of their phones, probably giving my name to Google in order to discover whatever they could discover about me, since I hadn't appeared alongside them on the nominations list published in haste in the *Federal Gazette* the previous week by the new government, on the list that had been checked over for publication, on the list that in theory was meant to pacify the black students, the indigenous students and the white students who were in conflict in the country's universities, but which, after it was confirmed and released to all the media, ended up having exactly the same effect as throwing petrol

19

onto a bonfire. And then I felt ready to give at least a partial airing to the ghosts occupying my thoughts, ghosts that had also been those times when I felt uncomfortable being who I was, raised on the idea of being from a black family, an idea that became my identity, but moulded into a phenotype that jarred brutally with that identity, two factors that, when combined, expelled me forever from the generalisations of the game of he's black and he's white, giving me a huge non-place to manage, ghosts that made me, even according to the astonishing short-sightedness of the new government, simply the most convenient person to be there.

I have retained no memory of what I said at the start of my speech, but I do remember the moment when, after a few minutes, noticing in their eyes that, like me, they weren't quite sure what they were doing on that commission, cutting through our ritualistic first interaction, I took a deep breath and said I only had the authority to appear before the eight of them because there'd been a day, an unforgiving August the tenth nineteen eighty-four, which, despite the years that had passed, continued to spin about in my head, a whirlwind in an eternal present, a day when I witnessed and experienced as I'd never witnessed and experienced before all the cowardice of the hierarchisation of skin colours practised in Brazil, all the cowardice of a psychological massacre, of a psychic disturbance of broad social reach, and which wasn't going to be over any time soon, a day that had left me crazy for a good while, but afterwards had made me react, first violently, and then with some clarity. That was when the eight of them started to listen to me.

Sitting here on this plank-style wooden bench, one of those ones you still see in church community halls in neighbour-hoods on the periphery of the city, for the first time in so many years, it's obvious that what I'm feeling is a fear of this place, the Little Goat, better known as Billy's Xis, the snack van serving meat and cheese 'xis' sandwiches on the plot of land at the corner of Bento Gonçalves Avenue and Humberto de Campos, the street with the state school where I studied until sixth grade, where I received ear-slaps, noogies, shoves from behind, trips, toe-kicks in the back, blows to the neck, at recess, on the way out of class, at school parties, where I took two proper beatings, beatings that, in hindsight, ought to have been significant moments in my learning about the fragmentation of the pre-adolescent moral code in the general trajectory of adolescence, but which, besides the physical pain, taught me nothing, least of all about being in the position of somebody who's been defeated, somebody who can't avoid feeling the acid rain of humiliation coming down upon them, humiliation at having failed to be quick or aggressive enough, and where I got stabbed with pencil points, which sometimes broke and stayed embedded in the flesh of my forearm, and where I was hit with a balloon full of piss without having any way to react because the guy it came from was with five other guys and he was also holding a serrated blade in his hand, looking me straight in the eye and daring me once and for all to throw the brick I was holding or turn around and get out of there immediately if I didn't want to die or wind up crippled, the same school where I once went completely out of control and knocked a kid down with a haymaker punch, and where, more out of shock than technique, I doled out a well-placed leg sweep to another boy who out of nowhere called me son of a bitch Galego blondie, a trip that made him lose his balance, fall and hit his head and spend a few seconds unconscious. But my fear isn't due to Billy himself, that's the billy-goat Fernando, owner of the van, a friendly sort, a good guy, like his two employees, Salete and Mara, both good people too, nor because of the van's being located on that plot of land on the south side of Bento Gonçalves Avenue, the hardcore side of Bento, the side where the hill is, at the foot of the hill, the side of the favela, the unpaved streets, the open-air sewers, nor is it because of the civil police, the military police, the army all patrolling by in their vehicles, watching the kids on the street, even riding up onto the sidewalk, braking hard on this gravel of the car park to give them a bit of hassle, demanding to see their papers, slapping them around, nor is it because of the local cartel lieutenants, guys half a dozen years older than me, who come down here to get a beer, eat a xis with chicken hearts and egg, best in the neighbourhood, leaving that suspense in the air, because they arrive all calm, their guns more or less in view, and eat with their eyes peeled, scanning sidelong every person there, nor is it because of my having a cop for a father, an important cop no less, a big name in the Rio Grande do Sul police force, the big boss of all their forensic investigators, a brand I carry on my forehead and which is perfectly visible for a lot of people who come here, a mark that, in theory, makes me kind of untouchable, because you don't, not around here, fuck with the son of a policeman lightly, but which, you never know, could also prompt an unexpected attack from somebody who doesn't like the police. No, I'm afraid of Billy's Xis Van because I'm afraid of being contaminated by this place's way of thinking and talking, I'm afraid of ending up taking pride in this neighbourhood, of being just one more streetwise kind of guy doing the rounds down here, just one more guy who doesn't care if he's going to spend his whole life in the neighbourhood, is going to die in the neighbourhood, I'm afraid of getting used to Salete's chumminess, to Mara's jokes, to the mute violence that is the macabre presence of the handful of lone street brats that are always showing up here, always kind of dirty, always at random, always keeping the required distance so as not to bother the customers, kids of nine, ten, eleven years old who Billy helps out, giving away a cheap toasted sandwich, a soda, and then conveying, subtly, which is kind of Billy's brand, that they're to get out of his sight, I'm afraid of thinking it might be cool to spend a night on one of these rough benches, wasting time with a bottle of guaraná in my hand, resigned to the insignificance that's the trademark of this place, used to it like Bighead, big-headed Cláudio, who just sat next to me, an old friend who's been stuck to me and Lourenço since we showed up on foot from over in Moinhos de Vento fifteen minutes ago, watching the merry-go-round of people circulating, just talking crap.

23

I only came here with my brother because Billy's is the xis burger place that's closest to my street, Colonel Vilagran Cabrita, whose surname, meaning little goat, was what indirectly gave the van its name, because tonight there was no way I could go straight home, because I need to eat a xis with chicken hearts and egg, I haven't been able to eat any solid food all day, and then, not being a big drinker, trying to take a few swigs of a beer, listening, sitting next to my brother, who's much more 'in' with the locals, him talking to the guys and girls who're always telling me oh your brother's supercool, a real solid guy, fuck, good people, man, Lourenço this, Lourenço that, man, comments that come as no surprise because ever since we were kids, within our invisible impervious bubble, even with my being the oldest, I was always watching that way he had about him, the way he fitted into parties faster than me, made friends more easily than me, was loved by other people the way I could never be loved, I was always watching, watching until one day I started to copy him, his mood, his casualness, two things I could barely understand but which I learned to perform convincingly enough to finally incorporate them into my own way of operating.

Bighead decided to have a go at Joaquim Cruz, who, four days earlier, on Monday, won the gold medal in the eight hundred metres in the Los Angeles Olympics, he's been talking about the guy non-stop for several minutes now. What it takes to get Bighead to shut up is the arrival of Ivanor with his turbocharged Chevette, famous for its golden paintwork and for being one of the frequent winners at the illegal Saturday late-night drag races down at the end of Ipiranga Avenue, the bit between Antônio de Carvalho and Cristiano Fischer. Ivanor gets out of the car and heads over. This is some impressive trio here, huh, he says, shaking Bighead's hand, mine, and then Lourenço's, The two brothers together, and in the presence of the neighbourhood gigolo-major, he concludes. Bighead having shut his trap was also due to the burden of being permanently in love with Kátia, also known as Mumu after that brand of light brown *doce de leite*, Kátia Doce de Leite Mumu, Ivanor's girlfriend, who gets out of the car shortly afterwards. Kátia walks up behind Ivanor and, without looking directly at any of us, says hi, just a curt hi, then she takes her boyfriend's arm and drags him over to the van. Bighead waits till the two of them are some distance away, Mumu just does me in, Bighead says, She gets more goddess-like every day, more gorgeous, how's that even possible. Lourenço says nothing, I say nothing, then Bighead resumes his slanders. You guys mark my words, Joaquim Cruz isn't getting one more Olympic medal in his life, He's got no humility, He's going to start to ease up, Even having all the perks of someone who lives in the US, The best equipment, The best trainers, Mark my words, Store's closed, It's not gonna be opening up again, he predicts. I can't follow the Olympics, I can't be bothered, Olympics in the US especially, I reply. Bighead gives me a disappointed look. But, get this, I reckon if this guy, a guy who's come up from nothing, from the poor part of Brasília, if he wants to be proud of being one of the big names in global athletics, that's his right, I'm totally in favour, I say. I don't agree, in the interview I saw yesterday on TV, he wasn't just being proud, He was arrogant, Athletes got to set an example, got to be humble, Doesn't matter what he's had to suffer through in his life, That old story about a poor young boy who came up from the slums in a country that shits on any sport that's not football, it doesn't give any fool who wins a gold medal at the Olympics the right to be arrogant. If you say so, I say, restraining myself so as not to leave the bounds of camaraderie and start a serious argument with him, because what he's saying has no basis in reality. If I could, I'd have been up in Los Angeles since the first day of these Olympics, says Lourenço. If I could, I'd have been in Los Angeles since the first day of my life, says Bighead. I'd have loved to be able to watch the basketball games, says Lourenço. A basketball guy like you, you'd be at all the games, you wouldn't miss one, says Bighead, kissing my brother's ass as usual. He also played basketball at school but like me he didn't keep it up. He idolises Lourenço because of how Lourenço's on the gaúcho basketball youth team, he catches rebounds and assists better than nearly anybody in Brazil in his category, and because he's one of the rare athletes with an athletic scholarship from the Grêmio Náutico União, the biggest social club in the city, and because he knows how to get along with the guys from Moinhos de Vento and Auxiliadora, the guys with money, the guys who'd never set foot here in Partenon, and can do it without getting an inferiority complex and with no aggression. You were born for basketball, brother, Bighead says. I'm not tall enough to play on the wing if I want to go pro, I'm not as good playing point guard, which would be my only option, Pretty soon now I'm done, Lourenço says. One metre eighty-eight isn't that little for a small forward so long as you're as good on rebounds and good on assists inside the key as you are, there'll always be a place for you in basketball, I say.

Salete calls our number. Lourenço and I get up to go collect our burgers. Bighead keeps our places. Salete hands over my xis with chicken hearts and Lourenço's xis with salad. You good, 'derico, Lourenço asks, You're calmer, and he takes the squirty bottles with ketchup and mayonnaise. I think I am, I say. We go back to the bench, where Bighead is waiting for us. You guys hear about Chump, Bighead doesn't even give us a chance to sit down. I don't think Bighead knows this, but Chump's had it in for me since that time in sixth grade when he pinched a nylon Parmalat promotional sport jacket of mine I totally loved, a jacket you could only get by collecting thirty Parmalat long-life milk cartons and then taking them to exchange at Zaffari on Ipiranga, a big store that at the time was the best supermarket in the city and a place my mother avoided because it was an establishment where you never saw a single black employee on the tills, at the bakery, at the butchers, working as a packer, collecting the shopping trolleys in the car park, on security, you never saw any dark-skinned people employed anywhere, nothing, my father didn't notice that and he still doesn't but my mother didn't hesitate and she still doesn't hesitate, if she can buy something someplace else she'll go buy it someplace else. Chump always said no, he claimed he'd traded in the milk cartons for the jacket just like me. But one day, when he wasn't paying attention, I took the jacket and checked, and showed him and everybody around the piece of almost imperceptible darning my mother had done on the right-hand seam of the jacket which had arrived

27

unstitched and which I'd only noticed when I got home and opened up the packaging. She'd used a burgundy thread that clashed with the brown, beige and orange of the jacket. I didn't stick with the fight because I got along really well with Chump's girlfriend at the time, Lídia, who was getting nervous about my insisting he was a thief. After that day, Chump stopped wearing the jacket to school. What, Chump got arrested, Lourenço asks while he spreads ketchup on his xis. No, the Zulu kid got together with this woman who owns one of those five funeral homes in Santana, one of the ones that's near the Institute of Forensic Medicine, He's a partner now, Can you believe it, He must be screwing the old lady, He's got to be screwing her, That coal-black kid of ours does like running honeytrap cons on filthy-rich old white ladies, says Bighead, he's got the knack like nobody else. You're not much different, Lourenço jokes. Seems he put two Opala station wagons converted for transporting coffins into service in the business, Bighead said. Must have stolen them, I said. And it seems he put in a good bit of cash too, But check it out, This time Chump's not going to make it, That old lady from the undertaker's is smarter than him, says Bighead. No way you can be a police notary, a partner in a scrap-metal dealership and a partner in an undertaker's, that's too much work for him to be putting one over on other people, I say. But mostly he's just a receiver of stolen motorbike parts, Lourenço puts in, chewing with his mouth open. I don't know where that con artist gets the money, I say. Yeah, Chump's in the bike game, nothing he won't do, Totally someone it's best to keep your distance from, says Bighead. At that moment Anísio pulls up at the roadside, right in front of us, with his white Yamaha

TT125. Engine on, headlamp on, without lifting the visor of his helmet, he beckons Lourenço over. Lourenço gets up, xis in hand, and goes to meet him. The two of them talk for almost a minute. Lourenço heads back. All right, I ask. All right, 'derico, Look, just finish your xis, he says, and checks the time on his wristwatch, Meet me at home in fifteen minutes, he says. I can tell from the expression on his face that now's not the time to be asking questions. We'll talk, Cláudio, I'll see you around, says Lourenço to Bighead. Take it easy, Bighead says. Lourenço takes two bites of his xis, tosses the rest into the bin, returns to Anísio, gets onto the back of the bike. The two of them head off into the neighbourhood, I can see they're still talking, and then, just a little farther on, right before the corner with my road, Anísio swerves to the left, mounts the central reservation, doubles back in the direction of the centre to turn, against the one-way system and with his headlamp off, onto Veríssimo Rosa. I go back to eating my xis, thinking about what might have happened, I don't say another word to Bighead. A few seconds later, Bighead tires of my silence and gets up and wanders over to some people he knows who just arrived. I think about asking for a beer, then decide against it. I finish my xis, get up, I give Billy a wave from a distance, he's got his radar on all the time, I head up Bento Gonçalves on foot, I go the slightly more than two hundred metres to my street, Cabrita, and head in.

From outside the house, I see that the living room lights are on. Contrary to what I'd expected, Anísio's bike is not in the front yard. I go in through the garage door. My parents are at an office party with my mother's colleagues, the people who

29

work with her at the National Institute of Medical Care and Social Security. I go up the stairs from the garage, I walk down the little corridor through the service area, through the kitchen, in the lunch room I leave my key and wallet on the sideboard, I go into the living room. My brother is sitting on the biggest of the three sofas and in front of him, on top of the central table, is a .32 calibre revolver. I need to hide that gun, he says without taking his eyes off the weapon. Is it Anísio's, I ask. It's Anísio's brother's, he replies. Well, so what's happening, I ask. Anísio snuck off with it, he says, And used it, he says, and he stops. You mean he shot someone, I say. Yeah, a guy, he says. What do you mean, I ask. I'll explain later, Now I've got to hide this gun, he says. Hang on, He shot someone and hurt them, I ask. He says he's not sure, Seems he hit the guy in the chest, Might have killed him, he replies. I try to keep my cool. And where'd he go, I ask. I don't know, He left me down at the corner, he said he'd make contact later, my brother says. I need to know what happened, Lô, Can you tell me, I ask. Later, Federico, Later, and he checks his watch, Dad and Mum are going to arrive any moment, he says and gets up, Do you want to help me, he asks. And it seems to me as though he doesn't want to touch the gun, that he's not able to touch the gun. I answer yes, I'll help. He suggests we hide it in the gap above the ceiling. I agree, I tell him to go to the garage to fetch the ladder and then try to find the flashlight, I say I'm going to take the used casings out of the gun and crush them in Dad's metal lathe and then chuck them away tomorrow on Ipiranga, into the Dilúvio canal. He says not to forget to clean the gun, to remove any fingerprints. I say yes, I'll clean it and put it in a plastic bag, one of those ones Mum uses for freezing food. He suggests we put it in one of those nooks it's almost impossible for anyone to get to. I agree, I say the gun can stay there for a while and we'll see about what we do later. He looks at me, he asks if we're really doing the right thing, if it's not idiocy to hide the gun at home. And realising that I'm starting to get nervous because in my head I'm starting to see the appearance of every conceivable consequence resulting from the decision to hide a weapon that might have been used in a murder under the roof of our own house, I tell myself wake up, Federico, wake up, you dumb lump, your brother's nervous, now's not the time to be chickening out, get this shit done fast and do it right, and I answer my brother that the best possible place for anyone to hide a gun so that it stays hidden is in the house of a cop, a guy who came to Porto Alegre aged thirteen from the deepest interior with his widowed mother and ended up getting himself two jobs while he was doing vocational training as a chemical lab assistant at the Parobé technical school, and studied like crazy, and went into the police, and started to work as a forensics expert and became the most dedicated expert the state police had ever seen, an exemplary guy, a guy above any possible suspicion, and I pick up the gun from off the central table and, in front of him, my brother, having grasped how risky all this is, I try to look as confident as I possibly can.

Good morning, said Micheliny, aged thirty-two, an aide in the People Management Secretariat in the Federal Civil Service, a career official assigned to coordinate the commission's meetings, the last person to come into the meeting room on the morning of that second day of work. The group returned the greeting. She sat down at the vast oval table, her back to the retractable screen that was already opened and receiving the glare from the ceiling projector. I must admit to you all, ladies and gentlemen, I'm feeling more comfortable today than at our introductory meeting last week, and she took her laptop out of the leather case that was on top of the table, opened it, The Planning Minister and the Minister of the Presidential Cabinet have finally reached a consensus about what the goals and aims of our commission are to be, she took the HDMI cable from the junction box built into the centre of the table, plugged it into the laptop, And I hope, truly, that I'm up to the mission they've entrusted to me, and up to your own expectations, she said. I'm sure you'll coordinate all the work very well, Micheliny, said Ruy, aged fifty-eight, head of the IT Division of the Ministry of Education, who has already had dealings with the Secretariat of Continuing Education, Literacy, Diversity and Inclusion. I second my colleague's comment, added Altair, aged thirty-eight, a diplomat who, since the new government came to power, has occupied a committee post in the Ministry of Justice's Secretariat for the Promotion of Racial Equality. Micheliny took a bundle of papers out of her case, removed the elastic band holding the nine smaller bundles together to make up the larger bundle, checked the positioning of the butterfly clips on each one, stood up and started to hand them around. WORKING GROUP FOR THE DEVELOPMENT OF PLANS TO CREATE A FEDERAL ADMINISTRATIVE APPEALS AUTHORITY FOR THE PURPOSES OF THE SELECTION OF BLACK, BROWN AND INDIGENOUS CANDIDATES FOR VACANCIES RESERVED FOR QUOTA STUDENTS IN FEDERAL PUBLIC EDUCATION AND FOR THE DEVELOPMENT OF SOFTWARE FOR THE EVALUATION AND STANDARDISATION FOR THE PURPOSES OF SELECTION IN THE FIRST ADMINISTRATIVE INSTANCE OF BLACK, BROWN AND INDIGENOUS CANDIDATES FOR VACANCIES RESERVED FOR QUOTA STUDENTS IN FEDERAL PUBLIC EDUCATION was what was printed on the cover sheet of the material she had just handed me. I didn't read the pages that came after, I just waited for the others to express their opinions.

And no one did, which surprised me. At that moment, in dozens of Brazilian public universities, as everybody in that room knew, students were attacking one another, verbally and physically, on account of the quotas for black, brown and indigenous students, a wave of provocations and attacks that began the same week the government took office promising to implement a new order, a new dynamic of governance that would interrupt the free fall of the country's economy, a wave that also coincided with the approval of the implementation of ethnic quotas by top-ranked public universities that some years earlier had refused to do just this, a wave that, in that year of two thousand and sixteen, ended up leading to an inflaming of spirits that was unprecedented.

First of all some black students went up against the brown students, the lighter-skinned blacks, who, to the black students' way of thinking, were insufficiently brown, they were 'bogus brown', as they'd been branded by some black and dark-brown students who now organised themselves into nuclei of black militancy and started going round in phenotypical verification patrols through the campuses of various universities, light-skinned brown students with no phenotypical features that might link them to the ethnic group of the blacks, brown students who didn't have, according to those who were part of the patrols, any sense of scale of what it means to live immersed to the very last hair on your head in the inhospitable geography of racial hierarchy in Brazil, what we now call 'Afro-convenient' brown people, those who were merely inoffensively tanned and who'd decided to pose as true deep-down blacks in order to exploit the opportunity and surf on the advantage of quotas. But then the black students and the brown students also joined forces against the students who called themselves light-skinned browns, but who weren't even light-skinned browns because they were really whites according to the assessment of the nuclei of black militancy, totally shameless whites who, taking advantage of the exclusivity of the criterion of racial self-declaration, getting themselves a few sessions in a tanning booth, applying self-tanner spray to their skin, perming their hair, getting lip injections, now claimed to be black, or even just swore they were a part of the black community, the grandchildren of blacks, great-grandchildren of blacks, while allowing their light skin to stay light, with no recourse to artifice whatever despite their skin being white, painfully white, a phrase coined in an essay entitled 'Painfully White' written by a black girl in high school from the Maré favela in Rio de Janeiro and published in the Manguinhos Library's *Sector X* magazine and later republished in a columnist's slot in *O Globo* newspaper at the start of that year, students who the black students from the patrols accused of being nothing but scammers, white criminals who went beyond the Afro-convenience of the totally poker-faced light-skinned brown people, and who surely must have been hoping to explode forever the system of racial quotas implanted, with such difficulty, in twenty-first-century Brazil.

Not a month after the first accusations and radicalisations on the part of the black students came the explosion, with white students who claimed membership of any of the countless groups motivated by racial intolerance and inspired by the theories of white supremacy that started to bubble up on the internet following the attack on the Twin Towers in New York on September eleventh two thousand and one, attacking quotas, who were against the black, brown and indigenous students who benefited from the quota system, and white students who weren't part of any group founded on an argument of racial supremacy, but who, being fans of

35

the discourse of meritocracy, were staunch opponents of the system of racial quotas for students of any phenotype, against black and brown students, and white students who had initially been in favour of the quotas but who, having shared a classroom with quota students, had become opponents of quotas, against black, brown and indigenous students, and some more or less moderate white students, who said that they weren't sure whether a university was the proper place for an Indian, against indigenous students, and white students who weren't moderate at all and said openly that if Indians wanted demarcated lands then they should damn well stay in their demarcated lands, not come here complicating the lives of civilised people, against indigenous students, and white students averse to quotas against white students favourable towards quotas, and white students who had been against quotas but who, having shared a classroom with black quota students, had now come out in favour of quotas, against white students who were opponents of quotas, and black students against white students, in response, indigenous students against white students, in response, and, in response, light-skinned brown students against black students and dark-skinned brown students.

It was surreal that what the new government had decided to present to these people willing to participate in the commission was this proposal for the creation of a piece of software for figuring out who was sufficiently black, brown or indigenous to reap the benefit of the quotas. It had to be a joke. Micheliny, however, wasn't treating it like a joke, and after distributing the materials to each of the members she sat back down, she thanked Ruy for his collaboration, as he had worked with the secretariat team to hammer out the finer details of the material in the chapter on the development of the said software. Ruy said thank you for the polite acknowledgement, and it was more than visible in his expression that he thought the proposal for this piece of software a very good proposal indeed.

Micheliny, Just one thing I'm not sure about, said Demétrio, aged thirty-five, federal public defender, a doctoral student in civil procedural law at the University of Brasília, Developing the parameters for a piece of software to facilitate the evaluation of candidates who're asking to benefit from quotas in just these few months the commission is in operation, Is that really doable, he asked. It's more than a piece of software for expediting the evaluation of candidates for quotas, Dr Demétrio, it's a piece of software that will give greater certainty and greater legal security to the matching of vacancies with quota students according to race, The software is going to standardise criteria, It's going to move us away from the subjectivity inherent in our current quota-student selection panels, that subjectivity which is the great enemy of our quota policy, It'll do away with the awkward situations to which students of intermediary phenotype, the light-skinned brown ones especially, are exposed when they appear at interviews for the verification of their racial self-declarations. And yes, Three months, with more frequent meetings in this month and then meetings more spaced out in the two later ones, will be enough, replied Micheliny. In any case, it's a curious idea, remarked Demétrio. Here at the secretariat, Dr Demétrio, we think it's a brilliant idea, And perfectly feasible, I really do want to be clear about that, said Micheliny. Ruy suggested we start reading the material. And, complying with the suggestion, Micheliny began projecting her presentation onto the screen in front of me, a presentation of the same text she'd already distributed, and she asked if anyone would volunteer to read it aloud. Ana Beatriz, aged thirty-two, designated auditor at the Ministry of Transparency and Federal Comptroller General's Office, volunteered. I tried to follow along with her reading on the projected text, but I just couldn't do it, I was too dazed, seeing myself there, raised up into the role of a supplier of altogether imprecise defining parameters for the programmer-technicians of a piece of software for judging physical features, skin colours. Eventually the dazed feeling ended up turning into total disconnection.

When Ana Beatriz finished reading, Micheliny thanked her for her contribution and set twenty minutes for a round of questions and answers. I have two questions, said Andiara, aged thirty-nine, recently promoted to federal circuit prosecutor for the First National Zone. Do please ask them, Dr Andiara, replied Micheliny. Just Andiara's fine, Micheliny, said Andiara. I think we can all drop the formality, said Ana Beatriz. Everyone agreed. Great, Andiara, said Micheliny, What questions do you have. The first is, I was interested to know if our aim is to put an end to racial self-declaration, Is that the committee's aim, asked Andiara. Not exactly, What's going to happen is that everyone who requests inclusion among the quota beneficiaries will have to transmit, via the computer program or phone app, a video recorded on their phone, under specific lighting conditions, replying to questions that are also to be defined by our commission, questions that will be applied in a standardised way to all candidates who seek to benefit from the quotas, And so self-declaration is being absorbed into this procedure, It becomes implicit, I don't really think that, put in this way, it necessarily suggests it's being eliminated, Ms Andiara, And I think, in practice too, it won't be, Micheliny concluded. Another thing, This demand for childhood photos, for photos with their biological parents, Really I think that's going too far, There are other things that are going too far too, of course, But that demand seems particularly flagrant to me, The candidate might not have photographic records of their childhoods, Besides which the phenotypes of the parents might not coincide with those of the candidate, And that's just one of many possibilities, said Andiara. These are matters that should be defined by the commission, Micheliny emphasised. What we're talking about is a colour-spectrum metric, Mauro, forty-two-year-old associate director of the Foundation for Applied Economic Research, jumped in. There's no way you can create a colour-spectrum metric, a negrometer, an official racial scale you can just plug into a computer program, and he twisted himself in his chair pulling towards him the pad of paper with the insignia of the secretariat that had been supplied to each of us, While Ana Beatriz was reading, he said, I had a look at the Suvinil Paints page just to check what names they apply to the range of colours they sell, and I jotted some of them down, only a few, the ones that could be variations of what you call light-skinned brown, medium brown and dark-skinned brown, he picked up the notepad, The intermediate light tones are, he straightened his glasses on his nose, Cream, Marshmallow, Lychee Cocktail, Lemon Sorbet, Light Almond, Fair Skin, Sunbeam, Crème Caramel, Maranhão Sand, Old Straw, Egg Custard, And the medium and darker ones, Earth Track, Cashew, Tanned Skin, Banana with Cinnamon, Walnut, Chestnut, Bronze, Cane Sugar, Firewood, Clay, Brick, Aged Silver, Raw Sugar, Caramel, Brazil Nut, Natural Cinnamon, Nutmeg, Clove, Ground Coffee, Powdered Chocolate, Powdered Cinnamon, Mahogany, Máte Gourd, Semi-Bitter Chocolate, All these names, and you can check for yourselves on the site later, can be colours of human skin, Is that really where this commission is headed, overdoing the sarcasm. No classification is ever going to be perfect, but it needs to be done, Per the directive from the government, somebody's got to take on this responsibility, Micheliny countered. Anything suggested along those lines seems unconstitutional to me, Mauro said firmly. And then all the others' objections came, all at once.

It was quite a few minutes before Micheliny was able to regain control of the meeting by proposing that we make our statements one by one, in alphabetical order, and further arguing that if the proposal for the software was not a good one and needed to be improved upon or abandoned, that the commission should first deal with the methodology for the development of the software devised by the secretariat and only then present their dissenting opinions and suggest appropriate adjustments. I'd so hoped she wasn't going to say that.

Ignoring the sequence of speakers that Micheliny had suggested, Ricardo, aged twenty-three, graduating student from the faculty of civil engineering at the Federal University of Paraná, nominated by a group of dissidents from out of the group who were running the National Students' Union, seeing as the members of the official NSU had refused to nominate anybody to be a part of the commission, asked whether it wouldn't be better to take the word brown out of the law entirely. Micheliny said yes, there were people from the black movement, a small number, who supported that idea, and who were asking for the legislation to be altered to leave only the black and indigenous people in the government's affirmative action legislation in relation to the system of racial quotas, but that such an exclusion was out of the question, because there were quite solid historical rationales for the presence of the black and brown students in the policy of quotas, historical rationales that she enumerated succinctly, rationales that he, Ricardo, who had agreed to be there to represent the country's students, surely knew.

By that point I could have ventured to say that these were no longer individuals, they were just people with no significance in the big picture of the bureaucracy of the state, people who, ultimately, represented nobody. I knew so many guys like them and I could identify their types from a distance, nineteen years in Brasília had given me that knack and had also imprisoned me in a network of relationships that obliged me to deal with certain requests when those requests were made by important partners, by directors of non-governmental bodies who contracted my services, recommended my assistance to

41

other people and gave me financial support when I showed up anxious in front of them with ideas on which nobody of sound mind would bet a centavo. Among the reasons that led to my participating in that commission, the decisive one was the request from an old friend, the president of a foundation in São Luís do Maranhão, who, not being in the best of health when she was sounded out to join the commission herself, and even though she had some sense of the scale of that particular white elephant, thinking somebody had to sacrifice themselves to prevent the direction of the meetings heading ultimately towards catastrophe, called me to say I was the only person in Brasília to put the brakes on that whole adventure and that she was going to put my name forward as well as mobilise some other organisations involved with projects for the inclusion of young people in leadership spaces, the better to apply pressure requesting my presence in the group. I couldn't refuse and I didn't. Nineteen years taking part in commissions of all kinds convened by organs of the government, or by organisations linked to the government, had taught me a fair bit about the rules by which such groups operated. One of those rules was that interdisciplinary working groups, with very few exceptions, were not to be mistaken for spaces in which it paid to get too committed. Politicians only create commissions in order to demonstrate to our anaesthetised society that they are taking some sort of action whenever that anaesthetised society decides to rouse itself and apply some pressure of its own. This was why, if I had to state what those commissions devoted to general Brazilian public service headquartered in the Brasília I knew actually were, in a word, I would say they were gatherings of people who were mainly experts in blowing their own horns, and in which somewhere between sixty and seventy per cent of participants weren't concerned with making too great an effort, and in which it was possible to identify a standard pattern that included four basic types of involvement: the first, that of the overseers, the puppets who headed up the work and whose careers were directly linked to the commissions' successes, and so were unwavering in their commitment, the second, the rare members who were genuinely interested in the results of the work, who ended up finding it disgracefully frustrating to have wasted their time on meetings and blah-blah when the result of the work was not the result that their convictions, their interests, called for, or when it was not the result that the people they ultimately represented were expecting, leaving them feeling personally culpable for the commission's failure, the third type of involvement characterised by those members who were technically necessary for the advancing of the work, those who spent a good part of their days outside the meeting room, taking advantage of the coffee that had been provided, keeping up with social media, but who knew that when they were called to contribute they were the only ones really in a position to say something that might close down everyone else's arguments, and finally comes the fourth group, those who joined the commission purely by virtue of being in the civil service, and, as public servants, in the merry-go-round of allocations wherever they were occupying a position, ended up being called to fill some vacancy on some commission simply because it's Buggins's turn, they had no trouble feigning involvement, allowing the leaky boat to keep floating along on the current, and they were equally able when the notion took them to intervene at just the right moment and even change the whole course of what was happening, change it either because this was necessary or for sheer sadistic amusement. If I couldn't count myself among the committee members with a direct interest, neither did I feel myself to belong to the group of participants content to allow the boat to float with the current, especially after Micheliny distributed her printouts making reference to the creation of the software right on the cover. So now I saw myself leaning towards the cadre of the technical experts, the ones who keep the project running, being somebody who, in that cascade of information, might still tell it like it is, provide the decisive piece of data, the decisive statistic. But the role of vital participant, of technical expert, wasn't any more appealing to me, maybe mine wasn't a leading role at all, maybe I was more playing the role of caretaker in a script featuring Micheliny in the lead, playing the building manager, with Ruy as her deputy and me as a secondary character who was mainly absent, invisible, but in a position to step in and play technician if it became necessary, if his back was against the wall, as indeed it would transpire after our mid-morning snack break, a break during which I twice helped myself to some of the chamomile tea that was there in a thermos, and I attacked two chicken drumsticks, two cheese-breads and two slices of chocolate-covered carrot cake. I had skipped breakfast, now was the time to make up for it. And I stood in a corner looking through that ninth-floor window at the dystopian and monotonous expanse of that same old Brasília.

When we returned for the second part of the meeting, Micheliny turned on the voice recorder, as she had warned she would do before the break, and reminded us that we would each, in alphabetical order, have precisely ten minutes to lay out whatever was most critical and urgent in our minds on the subject of quotas and the overcoming of inequalities on the basis of racial phenotype in Brazil, because, based on our declarations, she and her team would, within the methodological framework presented earlier, organise subtopics within our topics of discussion and deliberation for future meetings.

Altair went first. He talked about the childhood he had spent with his widowed mother who forbade him, her only kid, to leave their apartment that was in a housing project in the outskirts of the city of Belo Horizonte to play with the other children from the block, from the street, from the neighbourhood, he talked about the TV soaps they'd watch sitting together on the sofa and about when, while he was still a child, he was surprised not to see any black actors on the screen, not in the main parts and not even in the supporting ones, he said TV soaps were a source of education, they were the primary form of schooling for a lot of people in Brazil, that it was a crime not having the cast of each programme, each commercial, consist of at least fifty per cent black and brown actors, because television was a public service that depended on public grant and should therefore be run in such a way as to better cater to the public interest. He talked about the low self-esteem of black Brazilian university students, he compared them to the Angolan and Mozambican exchange students who came to Brazil to study and who, in emotional terms, even in terms of their self-image, on account of knowing where they came from, knowing their ancestry, the history of their ethnic group, arrived here with a huge advantage over the majority of black Brazilian students who, being descended from people who had been enslaved, had had their identities dissolved, suppressed by colonialism, by the mercantile process of enslavement. He said he'd had a black boyfriend once, a foreign student he was with for five years, whose skin was really, very dark black, and he confessed that, despite the intimacy he'd shared with this guy for so long, he was never able to not notice and so refrain from showing surprise whenever he went in, for example, to a restaurant largely patronised by people with light skin and was faced with a black person sitting at a table as a customer. He said he'd ended up working on that in therapy, he wanted to eliminate that sort of gaze from his life, but that he hadn't been able to lose it. With some emotion in his voice he asked how this was possible, how could people be disliked, feared, excoriated for the colour of their skin, how could this foul culture, which got into children's heads and ruined everything that was in there at the very start of their existences, how could it be allowed to continue, how could whites, whites like him, control everything, inventing some story about how racism wasn't real and on top of everything manage to win the support of a good portion of the black population in the process. He closed by saying that, if a skin-colour spectrum metric was indeed implemented, then it was time to use it in favour of the dark-skinned, use it to ensure that all spaces, or at least public spaces, would be filled with more dark-coloured people, he said that the commission did indeed need to cater to the demands of the factions within the black student movement that were demanding a radical solution, so that black people would be more present in both our universities and the civil service. Micheliny asked if he wanted to add anything else. Altair said no. Micheliny reset the voice recorder, told Ana Beatriz she had ten minutes.

In my own identity I don't experience the identity of black people, I had a white-indigenous mixed-race grandmother on my father's side, but even as a little girl I never felt tied, by blood or anything else, to any black ancestry, Not that I'm trying to distance myself from my own blackness, But the fact is that blackness did not exist in my upbringing, An upbringing that was not one of privilege, not upper middle-class and certainly not wealthy, I want to make that absolutely clear, And I guess if I'd been brought up with black culture more present, with black religiosity closer to me, maybe my identity wouldn't be so compatible with my phenotype, with my siblings' phenotype, which is a white phenotype, said Ana Beatriz. You feel white, asked Altair. Yes, replied Ana Beatriz. You don't feel mestiça, Altair insisted without realising the redundancy of his question. When I look at myself in the mirror, I don't see anything mestiça about myself, Do you see a mestiça when you look at me, she asked. I see a white person, replied Altair. That's it, even though I know that, according to origin-based criteria, I'm mestiça, I'm mixed-race like all we Brazilians are, I keep thinking about how I would handle the possibility of self-declaration, according to the criterion of phenotypical appearance, and the whole one-drop rule, if I was phenotypically brown, And I don't know what I'd do, she said, It's just I don't live in the social reality of black people, indigenous people, It's just that I'm white, said Ana Beatriz. Have you never been in a relationship with a black person, asked Altair, who clearly hadn't understood the dynamics of this group activity. One time I was really into this dark-brown boy when we were on a school trip, one of those trips where they hire a load of buses and kids from lots of different year groups go together, And I couldn't take my eyes off him, But my girlfriends discouraged me, they said he was too short, and I fell for their line, But I knew it wasn't to do with his height, their disapproval was really because of his dark skin, she said. Then she repeated a lot of what Altair had said, only she emphasised the budgetary bias, since, as she insisted on mentioning three times, she was from the Federal Comptroller General's Office, and, being from the Federal Comptroller General's Office, she could assure us that spending public money on black people, making compensation for the country's historic debt to them, was a most intelligent way of allocating public resources.

Even though she knew that Micheliny was going to monitor the time she took to speak, Andiara put her phone on the top of the table and activated its stopwatch. I think we need to keep valuing self-declaration, racial self-identification, because that's the only thing that's one hundred percent in accordance with the prevailing federal constitution, The right to racial self-declaration is a right that must be preserved and protected, And if some devious person defrauds it, the devious person who did the defrauding should be made legally accountable, But if a person sees him- or herself as black, brown-black, no matter how light their skin, this should be respected, she picked up the glass of water, took a sip, Some people say that any defining of parameters leads to prejudice, That every group has its parameters, that they're unassailable, But I don't think that's how it is, In Brazil when a person thinks of themselves as black, because they're from a black family, even if they're really light mestiço, and takes on, with this self-proclaimed identity, all the emotional and cultural stress that will assail them owing to the prejudice directed at the group to which they've linked themselves, I don't see why society shouldn't, through the parameters of social identification, unlike those of identity, see them as black, said Andiara. My dear Ms Andiara, I'm so sorry for interrupting, but it was precisely during this recent period when the criterion of self-declaration was prevalent, with merely claiming blackness being sufficient to qualify for full support from the Prosecution Service and the Ministry of Justice, that such flagrant injustices took place, with white people passing for black, which injustices brought us to where we are now, driving the very blackest students to anger and so leading to the war we're seeing in our universities today, said Micheliny. Well then, let me be more objective, Because I'm of the opinion that verification interviews, no matter whether they're the pre-emptive kind or the kind for assessing the truthfulness of self-declarations, should evaluate to what extent blackness influences the candidate's life, So I say again, skin-colour parameters, facial-feature parameters, these aren't sufficient, There are some self-declarations that can seem deceitful, false, but aren't, because even if the candidate knows that other people don't see them as black, differing as they do from one of their parents' phenotypes, they see themselves as black, and here she looked at Micheliny. Four minutes, Ms Andiara, replies Micheliny, though she knows Andiara is monitoring her own time. I think it's important to note that recent attempts have already been made at assembling charts of physical characteristics, phenotypical standards, for the purposes of evaluating and selecting candidates, In general, they feature three columns, The first, phenotype, listing shades of skin, types of nose, of lips, of gums, of teeth, of jaw, of cheekbone, types of forehead, of skull, of hair, of beard, tonality of the sclerotic coat, The second column for descriptions that take the person's so-called Negroid characteristics as a reference point, If that's melanoderma, black skin, then black to what degree, If it's phaioderma, brown skin, to what degree, And if, as it happens, it's leucoderma, white skin, then to what degree there too, And if it's a short nose, to what degree, If it's a flat nose, to what degree, If a wide nose, to what degree, And so on and so forth, With the third column being a function of the second column, itself having three internal columns, three sub-columns, corresponding to level A-1, level A-2, level A-3, These attempts having been administratively or legally challenged, and cancelled, That's it, Thank you, said Andiara, concluding her statement. Micheliny thanked her, she reset her recorder, she called on Demétrio.

Demétrio said he agreed with Micheliny about the problem with committees being their subjectivity, he said there were loads of committees for confirming the phenotypes of quota candidates that were made up entirely of white people, some of whom didn't have the slightest idea of what parameters to employ in order to assess the cases being considered, but that he couldn't accept the idea of a cybernetic evaluation either, which, as he imagined it, would use facial recognition technology configured in a Lombrosian fashion to recognise ethnicities in a country where the ethnic groups were already all mixed up. Lombrosian lombroso looking, I jotted down. Then he talked about his PhD and about how contemporary trial proceedings would condemn any state-sanctioned procedure involving fundamental rights being handed over to the management of a piece of artificial intelligence and he brought his talking to a stop before his ten minutes were up. Micheliny looked at me, said it was my turn.

I'll be brief, I said, But I wish everyone would please stop using the term race tribunals, It's a term used by racists who want to put an end to quotas altogether, I stressed, This commission mustn't give in to folks like that, and when I realised I was hitting the tabletop with the side of my stretched-out, tensed-up right hand, I stopped, relaxed my hand, and relaxed, The problem with the quota system isn't in the scope for subjectivity in the decision-making process during interviews held to verify the racial characteristics of quota candidates, With the greatest respect to my fellow committee members who have accepted that theory, the fact is that it's also a talking point beloved of racists who want, I say again, to screw over the quota system, What we have to understand is that wherever a judgment is made, whether legal or moral, it makes no difference, there will always be considerable scope for subjectivity, for personalities, for prejudices, for what is called, in the legal world, discretionary power, We've got people from the Law here, and I looked at Andiara and then at Demétrio, You people who're in the Law know about this, In the legal world no objectivity is ever undeniable, That's a part of the dynamics of any judgment, Last year, this federal judge from down in Porto Alegre explained this to me, He explained it using these exact words, and here I concentrated to retrieve what he had said from my memory, The subjective, a subjective reading, must be testable and provable, if it can be tested and proved then it is valid, That's what this commission has to put down on paper and disseminate to people, I said. When you put it like that it seems so simple, said Ana Beatriz. Objectivity in the everyday practice of the Law and of all its branches isn't perfect, Ana, why should it be with regard to quotas, I said, That's what I'm trying to tell you all here, Which is why, looking further ahead, I don't see how a piece of software can take the place of people, of the subjectivity that is inherent in those interviews, I don't see how this program could increase legal security or legal certainty, What's going to happen, and you don't need to be a genius to predict this, is that this appeals committee, this body that's going to consider appeals, apparently with its headquarters here in Brasília, isn't that right, It'll be born destined to be always overwhelmed, I concluded. Frankly, I think a lot of phenotypically white people who don't make it through the software selection aren't going to bother to appeal, And I think that could already be a big deal in itself, said Micheliny. Subjectivity can be reduced, but not eliminated, I said, Going round and round this question is just going round and round a false dilemma, A computer program can't eliminate that margin of subjectivity which will always be inevitable, and here I shut up. You've still got five minutes, said Micheliny looking at me with just a hint of anger. I fell for her bait, I resumed talking. Once I saw this play at the Theatro São Pedro down in Porto Alegre, the play was called *Ghana*, I said, There were only two actresses performing on the stage, two lead characters, and from offstage there was a male voice, which was the voice of an agent, an intermediary, who only talked to them on the phone and represented a businessman who'd decided to invite the two women to spend a few days together in a hotel in an isolated part of Ghana, in Africa, an enormous hotel that would be rented out just for them, the holders of two revolutionary patents, valuable patents for two programs, two revolutionary bits of software, one of which would replace judges and courts, reaching verdicts with an unprecedented precision and degree of justice, and the other which would replace psychologists and psychiatrists, likewise getting good results on an unprecedented scale, thereby democratising people's access to two essential services, services that do substantially define the quality of relationships in contemporary societies, For them to meet and talk about the possibility of a fusing of the two programs into a single one, and he offered them a good amount of money to do this, Money they'd earn just for meeting and talking for a few days, And at the end, which was kind of abrupt, it was revealed that the agent who was talking to them on the telephone was also a computer program and that their presence in that hotel, subjected to sporadic conversations with the alleged agent, was no more than a test that the government of a country the play never named had decided to carry out in order to assess the efficiency and effectiveness of a program devised to influence leaders and govern nations, Apart from that simple resolution, the final conversation between the two women and the voice off, as transmitted through the telephone on speakerphone, was a quite unique piece of dialogue, And, if I remember correctly, it seemed to be pointing the audience to a reading kind of like you just can't take a shortcut, humanity can't just forget about humanity, The hotel was a kind of metaphor for the nightmare of creation, of invention, forever subject to the temptation to reify, and, seeing that I was managing to have an impact on some of the committee members, I was left feeling exposed and foolish for having shared so much and having talked so quickly and enthusiastically without managing to maintain my clarity and objectivity the way I'd done before Micheliny said I still had five minutes left. You've got another thirty seconds, Senhor Federico, said Micheliny, and that little spark of anger was still there in her eyes, and I was starting to like her. You can move on to Mauro, I've already said what I had to say, Micheliny, I said.

A large portion of white society doesn't want to see black people up on their feet, They want the blacks to remain subjugated, enslaved, For a large portion of whites the presence of a black person in certain places shatters the sacred harmony of the environment, This to me is the point, it's what made me want to be a part of this commission, began Mauro, And I'm really sorry, but I'm going to keep going back over the subject of the software, We have to ask ourselves how much the news that this commission of ours is going to spend hours arguing about the production of a piece of software for selecting black and indigenous quota students is just going to provide arguments for the racists, just as Federico rightly pointed out, he said. As you've seen in the material I passed around, the commission's deliberations will be submitted for public consultation, Micheliny interrupted. No, what it says in this material is that there's a possibility of that, Micheliny, a possibility that will remain at the discretion of one of the two ministers you report to, What I think, he said in a rhetorical tone of voice, what I think is this new government isn't going to consult with the public at all, And I'm sorry, I know you're committed, in a good sense, you're enthusiastic, but your bosses aren't going to expend all their energies on canvassing for public opinion on such a wasps' nest of a matter as this, said Mauro. Wasps' nest, I jotted down on my notepad. This commission has to proceed with great caution, the hotheads representing the students in the universities, right at this moment, that's what they're showing us, There's a very large number of Brazilians who don't understand quotas and, whether cynically or not, don't agree with quotas, If we hold a magnifying glass over the Judiciary, we'd see that the Judiciary doesn't understand quotas either, that a part of it doesn't even want to understand, You cited that judge from down south, Federico, but that guy, a guy with that sort of clarity is the exception, from what little I've seen, And I don't want to generalise, but yeah, there's a whole load of judges and a whole load of members of the Prosecution Service who won't swallow quotas, The Judiciary is white, And the what do you call it, the epistemic basis of the Law, It's Europeanised, It's white, said Mauro. White epistemic, I wrote down. There's this one judge who just recently on a TV debate was saying there isn't any ethnic conflict in Brazil, a judge who can't get out of his bubble of privilege and see reality, A black man reports an instance of racism, first the judge mitigates the occurrence and then in the sentencing he relativises, he says there was no intention to cause offence, Now I'm not in the Law either, but those acquittals make me crazy, or those mitigated convictions that occasionally show up in the news, with a sentence that convicts for using a racial slur when it should be convicting for racism, Mauro said, and then he stopped. You've still got four minutes, said Micheliny. For the remainder of his time, he discoursed about how necessary it was to find a way to get those who weren't black to show more solidarity with the struggle of the blacks.

Then it was Micheliny's turn. Gentlemen and ladies, So I'm the only person here who has really very dark skin, And I know, as perhaps none of you know, how complicated the codes of social and racial imbalance in our country are. I know how far any of the current, strictly intermittent relationships between certain racial groups actually are from provoking any sort of real reduction in the cruel racism we've been living with, and this cohabitation doesn't mean harmony, racism's right here, chromatic hierarchy is right here, And I know every one of you has their opinion about the appropriateness of the software and I imagine you even have some resistance to the creation of a federal appeals committee for standardising selection criteria, but I ask you to understand that something needs to be done to calm people down about this question of our quotas, which are supported by the Federal Constitution and are enshrined in law, but which need to be implemented correctly and need to function as intended, under penalty of the system's not being renewed in future by our representatives in Congress, There are many issues that concern me, so I'll try to be as comprehensive as I can in my approach, And I know a significant part of the black movement is arguing for a single national standard of judgment, that the criteria for judging who is brown-skinned and who isn't should then be valid for the entire country, disregarding the fact, for example, that somebody considered white in the Salvador of singer Margareth Menezes very likely wouldn't be considered white down in Gisele Bündchen's Horizontina, What do you all think of that, ladies and gentlemen, she asked and looked at each of us in turn, Because I'm in favour, she said. Racial identity and racial identification are cultural constructs within society, Micheliny, don't forget that, And Brazil is vast, said Mauro. Yes, but we're going to be retaining the criterion of social recognition, of how society perceives a person, we're just trying to establish a parameter for the official appraisal, And I do respect the position you're taking, Federico, but it's not only the racists who draw attention to the problems of subjectivity, There's a part of the black movement that's also demanding more objectivity and more transparency in the criteria of phenotype assessments, Those of us in the secretariat think the software in question ought to be capable of taking into account the particularities of the locations where the selection will be implemented, but this would significantly increase the number of very tiny details that'd need to be built into the cogs of the machine and so, I'd venture to say, would only elevate the risk of uncertainty in its operations, rendering impracticable the very sense of reliability upon which everyone, at some point, whether it's the racists or the historically oppressed, insists, said Micheliny. I had an intern who used to tell me she was black in her class at law school, white in the community where she lived, she lived in this seriously violent favela, was nicknamed Morena for her brown skin tone by her own family, a family in which her three brothers, born out of her light-skinned mestiça mother's second marriage to a white man, are much lighter than she is, said Andiara, That's the scale of the problem, That's what we have to keep in mind, she said. Micheliny nodded and went on, she ended up listing almost twenty additional points that were troubling her. After she had finished her presentation, she apologised for having exceeded the time limit that she herself had set and informed us that, at the end of Mauro's presentation, she had received a WhatsApp message from the advisors at the Presidential Cabinet Office notifying her that the news about the development of the software was going to be released in the following day's federal gazette and pointing out that we would have to be prepared, perfectly in tune, all nine of us, because the press was going to be on top of each one of us then, and she said to Ricardo that he had ten minutes.

Was Clara Nunes white, Jorge Amado white, asked Ricardo, beginning his statement, is Caetano Veloso white, Chico Buarque white, is the best woman footballer in the world, Marta Vieira da Silva, white, is the singer Gal Costa white, the rapper Marcelo D2 white, the singer Marina Lima white, Am I, with this hair and this nose, white, he asked, projecting his voice in a way that was totally excessive for a place like that meeting room, maintaining the attack posture characteristic of the student militants from every generation I've ever had the opportunity to meet, It's in the interest of the whites from the élite that the blacks argue among themselves the way they're arguing in Brazil's universities, it's in their interests that brown people don't start trying to pass themselves off as blacks, And I agree when he says, and he pointed to Mauro, there's no point waiting for the courts, And if you ask me there's no point waiting for the National Congress either, Because given the morons who're there at the moment, and the trend is for things only to get worse, the quota system isn't going to be renewed when it should be renewed, Unless some miracle happens, Everyone in this room knows that, The democratic political context is moving backwards in Brazil, There isn't, at this point, any salvation for the people, not through the action of public institutions, What there is, however, is a concrete threat against the people that's coming from and is posed by those same public institutions, Public institutions have become enemies of democracy, And this commission is proof of that, because the aim here, and I'm not even going to waste my time on this laughable software idea, is to establish a federal race tribunal, and he looked at me, sitting directly in front of him, with eyes that seemed possessed, pure rage, the guy was like an actor, Everybody here, including me, is privileged, We've managed to become insiders, we're among the lucky few in Brazil who benefit, The logic of the slave owners still applies, In the circles of command and authority, a black doesn't get in, And if he does, it's only one of them, two max, And that stinks, That's going to have to change, Quotas should be for sixty per cent to come from the black and indigenous population, Now that would be proper compensation, That would be real democracy, he said very loud. This kid's going to have a stroke, I thought. The academic community needs to be darker, And if making it darker means lighter people get kept out, then let them be kept out, he said. His Rio accent, from Baixo Gávea in the Zona Sul, as he seemed not to have lost his way of talking despite having moved away to Paraná, didn't suit his exasperation. His was the statement that excited me the most, but just the same, at a certain point, I started doodling on the notepad and switched off.

Ruy was the most predictable, he talked about the software, about what a cell-phone app version would be like, he said he'd like to see a national register on which the racial qualification of the candidates would be recorded, qualification was the word he used, he made the case that a national register would prevent somebody who'd tried to defraud the system over in Mato Grosso do Sul from being able to try again up in Piauí. Looking at Demétrio, he said he was a fan of facial recognition and that the software could start from the protocols used in facial recognition software while adding other elements, of course, and he promised it was going to be revolutionary, reminding us that the software would definitively keep the defrauders away, he said humans make mistakes and are inconsistent, but this software, even if it did perpetrate some injustices, which could be remedied by the appeals committee, would at least be consistent, and from what little he knew of the Law, consistency was justice. He talked so fast he didn't leave room for anybody to intervene, and he proved himself the most accomplished seller of ideas in the group. At the end he said his mother was mulatta and that he, despite his tanned white skin, thought of himself as true-mulatto, confiding, right away, that he couldn't understand why, from one moment to the next, the word mulatto, which was even in 'Aquarela do Brasil', that anthemic song known and loved in every corner of the planet, as even Caetano Veloso had pointed out the other day, had gone onto the list of words that were politically incorrect, he said that relating it to the word mule was ludicrous, that mulatto came from muwallad, which was the term used by the Arabs to refer to the mestiços born to Arabs with women who weren't Arabs when they invaded the Iberian Peninsula, and that even if it really had come from mule the term had been given another dimension by custom and usage, another connotation. He concluded his presentation with the statement I'm a mulatto and I'm proud to be mulatto. All that was left for Micheliny, who I'm sure didn't agree with that enthusiastic defence of the word mulatto, was to take a deep breath and wind up the morning's work notifying us that we should be back at 2 p.m. on the dot.

When everybody was already on their feet, having realised that instead of gathering up the material into her folder she was pulling out other bundles of printed papers, Altair asked if she wasn't going to be taking a lunch break. Micheliny said she'd be staying to organise the afternoon's activities. Ruy offered to help her. She replied that she wouldn't say no. And he stayed.

There was no one taking a leadership role, except perhaps Micheliny, which was only to be expected, but there was no one just playing caretaker either, as I'd thought there would be. I left a little frustrated but aware it was still too early to give anyone on the commission a label. In the hallway, Demétrio suggested a group lunch, but Mauro and Ricardo had other commitments and the others didn't seem very enthused. As we waited for one of the three elevators to come by, Ana Beatriz said she was really enjoying being a part of the group. Andiara was the only person who replied, she said something like I hope we go on making good progress like this throughout. The right-hand elevator opened with six people in it, another five would fit. Ricardo said he was in a hurry and stepped forward. Mauro said ladies first. Andiara said she could wait for the next one, she wasn't a big fan of crowded elevators. I said I'd wait for the next, too. Ana Beatriz got in. Demétrio hesitated, but then got in. Altair got in. Mauro looked at Andiara. She replied with a gesture to relax, it's fine, you can go. And he got in. The elevator door closed. Not ten seconds later the middle elevator opened without a single living soul inside. Andiara went in, and I went in. I looked at her, I said I wasn't sure whether I was going to have lunch, my stomach was still assessing the two slices of carrot cake. She laughed, said she'd also overdone it. I said I was thinking about getting a beer at the Bar Brahma in 201-South and asked if she'd join me for a beer. She nodded and said she could really use a beer.

Founded by German immigrants in the second half of the nineteenth century, the Leopoldina Associação Juvenil is considered the most élitist of all the social clubs in Porto Alegre and the most rigorous when it comes to the matter of nonmembers entering its premises. In order to gain access to its open parties, outsiders need to be accompanied by a member who informally takes responsibility for the non-member's behaviour within the club. My intention today, early this afternoon, had been to spend the evening at home, go to bed early, wake up early tomorrow, go for a run up to Redenção Park, do a few pull-ups, a few press-ups, a few sit-ups, but I got on board at the persuasiveness of Joel 'Fearless Fly', a super-smart guy who does crammer school with Lourenço, I got on board when he called me around two saying he had spare tickets for a party that was happening today, Friday, August tenth, at the Leopoldina, and, if I was interested, he could pass at least one on to me so he wouldn't be left so out of pocket, promising the party was going to be the best party because the music was being done by DJ Kafu, a guy from my brother's crowd who works in the studio at Rádio Ipanema and who's been making his name around the city DJing parties in posh clubs, playing rock music, surfer sounds and a

put together, I add. So anyway, How'd it go at the recruitment thing, he asks. All good, I reply. Any chance they could get you, he asks. I hope not, Last thing I want to do in this life is military service, I reply. I'm still not sure if I don't want to do it, he says. I change the subject. How are the classes going, I ask. Cool, he says. Cool, yeah, so you've been going, I ask. Yeah, No doubt, Next year I get my diploma, he says. Don't take too long, Lourenço, Dad and Mum worry, The old man doesn't show it, not like Mum shows it, but I think actually, of the two of them, he's the one who's most worried, This business of you getting held back a year over and over is making them crazy, I say. Message received, he says and he moves away, I'm going to have a wander round, See who's down near the back of the line, he tells me. His seeing who's down near the back of the line is, in reality, his saying I wonder whether Etel's coming to this party. Etel, the daughter of the Jews who own the main toy-store chain in the city, the girl who shows up unexpectedly at our place for little visits, fooling around with him, in his room, listening to the records she brings round, the girl who's totally messing with his head because they're a couple when they're at the house but out on the street, depending who she's with, mostly if she's with anyone she's related to or who's close to her family, who have no idea she's in love with a black kid, she pretends he's just some classmate from remedial school. Lourenço says their relationship's great as it is, that he knows how to go with the flow, that she's just another of those little rich girls who're into him because he does modelling work and walk-on bits in TV ads and stuff like that, but the truth is he likes her, and this secret little fling of theirs, which has been going on for a year already, is destroying him inside. I'll go with you, says Manoel. And they go.

I stay behind with the other five, just doing my own thing, just listening to the story Travolta is telling Lima, Rainer and Paulo André. Anísio seems vague, even less enthusiastic than I am. I let him be, Travolta's got a way with those stories, which tend to involve lots of fucking around, this story's about the first time he screwed the private tutor in maths, physics and chemistry who his mother, a well-known lawyer from a traditional Partenon family, a wealthy widow who could have got out of Partenon years ago but dismissed the idea of swapping the neighbourhood where she was born for anywhere else, and who said she wasn't going to put her hard-earned money into a pre-college entrance crammer for her son because crammer schools are all big-time scams, machines for printing money, hired in order for him, Eduardo Travolta, beloved son who wasn't much of a studier, to make better progress preparing to go to university, along with one other teacher for Portuguese, geography and history. I know the story already. It's almost at the end now, actually it's already finished, Travolta's just going back over the spiciest details, emphasising that coming on to him had been her initiative, that she was a nerd, big and wild, the determined kind of nerd who knew what she wanted and knew how to use a man whenever and however she wanted. No longer very entertained by his rehearsing of those details, which were doubtless new to Lima, to Rainer and to Paulo André, who were from Moinhos de Vento and from Auxiliadora, but which weren't new at all to the Partenon guys like me and Anísio, I look towards the front of the queue, of the queue that still hasn't started moving, and I see that my cousin Elaine is arguing with two girls, two girls who are with six other guys, all of them wearing Grêmio club shirts, except one, the strongest-looking one, who's in a K&K surfer T-shirt.

It isn't a Grêmio match day, but it's the eve of the eleventh, the day on which last December the Grêmio team won the Intercontinental Cup, the Toyota Cup, the day on which, every month, the Gremistas, en masse, go around in their club shirts to commemorate the historic victory. As it's a Friday, it's not surprising to see a group of friends who probably won't be able to meet up on the Saturday marking the occasion in advance at domestic barbecues, in restaurants, in bars, on the streets.

I take a few steps, I see Elaine wagging her finger in the face of the girl who, in addition to the Grêmio shirt, is also wearing a Grêmio cap. One of the guys, the one who's in a polo shirt with the club crest embroidered on the sleeves, puts himself between them, apparently trying to defuse the situation. The other five guys and the other girl, the one with the headband, just watch. Even from a distance, you can see from their posture that they're on their own turf and that this other girl, my cousin Elaine, is not. I head over. The guy who's in the polo shirt with the Grêmio crest embroidered on the sleeves takes hold of the shoulder of the girl in the cap and talks to her, but she doesn't move away, she isn't the least bit intimidated, on the contrary, she's as furious as my cousin. Apologise, go on, preppy girl, apologise, those are the first words I'm able with any certainty to hear coming out of Elaine's mouth. I speed up. Elaine realises the person approaching is me. What's going on here, I ask her. Would you believe it, Federico, this crazy girl walked right past looking straight at me and said to the other girl, that one there, that I need to learn to straighten my hair better if I want to come to a party at the Leopoldina, she said. I didn't say any of that, Isn't that right, Carol, This girl's tripping, replies the one in the Grêmio cap. The one in the headband nods. What happened is I walked past her, I looked at her like I'd look at anyone, and she pushed me, says the one in the cap, her eyes never leaving Elaine's. Hey pal, says the guy in the polo shirt with the Grêmio crest embroidered on the sleeves, I recognise you, You're Federico, aren't you, I'm Douglas, We know each other from junior basketball, I was on the team at the Farroupilha school, he says. Man, your friend was talking shit, She's going to have to apologise, I say. No way I'm apologising, says the one in the cap. Let's everyone calm down, says the guy in the polo shirt with the Grêmio crest embroidered on the sleeves, We'll be on our way, Let's go to that barbecue, You guys just be cool here, enjoy this party of yours, Can we just let it go, If we start arguing here in front of the club, their security people will call the police, it'll cause unnecessary trouble, They'll ban you, I'm not a member of the club but I'm from the neighbourhood and I know how those Leopoldina guys don't let any trouble start here in front of the club, and he looks at Elaine, Really I'm sorry if we offended you, It wasn't intentional, I can assure you you must have misheard, Sorry, he says and, taking the girl in the cap by the hand, he starts walking away from Elaine and me. I look at Elaine, and Elaine steps out of the queue, runs the few metres separating her from the guy in the polo shirt with the Grêmio crest embroidered on the sleeves and the girl in the cap, takes hold of her arm. Let go of me, filthy *maloqueira*, says the one in the cap. Elaine doesn't let go. Let's leave it, the guy with the polo shirt with the Grêmio crest embroidered on the sleeves says and he looks at me, Please, Let's settle this now, and he holds out his hand to me. Forget it, Douglas, There's no use talking to these people, says the guy in the long-sleeved Grêmio shirt, who's next to the girl in the cap. I put my hand on his chest, the chest of the guy in the long-sleeved Grêmio shirt, and I push. Don't do that, says the guy in the polo shirt with the Grêmio logo embroidered on the sleeves. Then the one in the long sleeves is on me. I kick him, put the sole of my foot in his stomach, a kick he wasn't expecting. He bends double with the pain. Something in my head explodes.

When the one in the long sleeves straightens up, with ludicrously perfect timing, I see Anísio appearing out of nowhere and, with a leap, the way only a guy like him who's so good in a fight knows how to do, he manages to execute a flying kick with both feet right in the chest of the guy in the long sleeves. The others react, I don't know how they managed not to notice sooner. And at the same moment I see Lourenço, Manoel and Travolta launching themselves at them. The girls start shouting, everybody around us starts shouting, Elaine manages to slap the face of the girl in the cap. The girl in the cap breaks out into the biggest racket. I listen to the guy in the polo shirt with the Grêmio crest embroidered on the sleeves asking for someone to call security. Then I'm on the guy in the long sleeves, who's still on the ground, I give him three punches in the face, he tries to defend himself, but he can't do it.

The club's security guards show up at the same moment DJ Kafu fires off the first number of the night on the other side of the wall, probably without the faintest idea of what's happening out here, it's 'Can You Feel It', by the Fat Boys, at full blast. One of the guards, the biggest of them, who happens by chance to be somebody we know from Partenon, Dante from Cefer, professional massive bouncer, famous across the city, shouts scram out of here, the pigs are going to show up and you'll all get it then, bunch of troublemakers, and he grabs my arm. Does your father know you're out here getting into fights, he asks, and then he looks at Lourenço, Get your brother out of here, and back to me, You're out of control, kid, Both of you get going, Just take advantage of the fact neither one of you's got hurt, and then an ultimatum, When the police get here I won't be able to do anything for you. Lourenço shouts a Let's do it to his friends. Each one of them runs in a different direction. Lourenço and I run to the corner of Félix da Cunha. Before turning towards O Parcão, I stop, I look back, I see the guy in the polo shirt with the Grêmio crest embroidered on the sleeves who ended up trading punches with Travolta and apparently got the worst of it, he's motionless, staring at me from a distance, the look in his eyes saying you could have avoided all this, you could have avoided it but you didn't.

Andiara and I took to having dinner together almost every night. She could have had the company of her colleagues from the Federal Prosecution Service if she'd wanted it, but since she was on paid sabbatical she didn't want to be wandering the Office of the Prosecutor General too much, what she really wanted was to make the most of her leave to finish the research and reading she'd been doing for the book about the relationship between economic law and human rights she'd been working on for a publisher of legal books in São Paulo for a year and a bit, a publisher whose editors were expecting the manuscript by the start of twenty seventeen. Phrases like I've got to get a grip, I really need to finish this book by next February, I need to start writing my missing chapters, I don't know if I did the right thing when I asked to join this commission, all of these kept coming out of her mouth randomly at varying intervals, some fifteen times at least, over the course of our conversation on the day we had four beers at the Bar Brahma during the lunch break of the commission's second meeting, which obliged me to ask how it was possible that anybody, while enjoying a period of paid sabbatical, could agree to take part in a government commission with a schedule of meetings as gruelling as ours when they ought to be really far away from the whole drag, from the bureaucracy, from all the activities of a federal circuit prosecutor, and focused on the writing of their book. She said it had been a rather un-thought-through initiative on her part, that it was a situation in which her emotional intelligence, so typical of people from Manaus, hadn't worked as well as it should have. The attorney-general had determined that, given the seriousness of the subject and of the possible repercussions of the directives coming out of the commission for racial quotas, it would be best to have a federal circuit prosecutor present, and she volunteered because she thought going to the meetings would stop her obsessing too much, would make her not immerse herself too much in the research and reading for her book, she thought the meetings might be a respite, that they'd give her a better perspective on what she actually needed to read and interpret, in addition to helping her with some of the most important points of the book, such as the valuing of work, the guarantee of a life of dignity and the principle of social justice in the current Brazilian economic order, she said she could see nothing more socially unjust than the crisis in the system of racial quotas for students at this moment. I countered that, in the bottomless pit of social injustices in Brazil at this moment, there were far more pressing things than the challenging of racial quotas in education. She replied with a grimace that kind of said look, mister social causes smartass, you can pay me later, and smiled.

We had an unusual connection, a connection that was established with unusual speed. That same night, without registering that it was a Tuesday, we went out to dinner at the Trattoria da Rosário on Parque Dom Bosco Avenue, in Lago Sul. We drank wine, we really got stuck into our conversation. We were in the middle of our second bottle when the waiter came over and brought us the bill. That was when we realised it was late and we were the last customers in the place. Andiara said thank you, and dinner that night was on her, and that I could pay for the next one, a proposition I accepted. While the waiter was replacing the cork in our bottle at my request, she asked whether we mightn't finish the remaining half someplace else. Someplace else, I asked. The waiter moved away. At your apartment, perhaps, she replied. I said it might be best to leave the wine and my apartment for another night. Without batting an eyelid, she said at least I wasn't ruling out the possibility of another night, she called over the waiter, who was starting to gather up the tablecloths, and handed him the bottle, saying it was a gift.

Two nights later, we went to dinner at New Koto in 212-South. When we ordered the third bottle of saké, she said she was glad to have met me. I replied that I felt the same. She asked whether I didn't want to go to the aparthotel where she was staying. I replied that perhaps it was too early for us to get involved. She asked whether there was somebody else. I didn't answer. She answered for me, saying I did have somebody else. You're terrible, Andiara, I said. I'm not terrible with everyone, Federico, Truth is, over the course of my life, I've been terrible with only a really small number of people, she said. I don't want you to misunderstand me, I said. She smiled. I'm only being terrible because you aren't going to screw me.

You're incredible, Are incredible, I was at the classic stage of drunkenness on saké in which I became incapable of articulating better sentences without first subjecting myself to a very great effort of concentration, and I smiled. She smiled too. It's complicated, I said. I've got no problem with just fucking, she said. I blushed. Look, Federico, You and I like each other, This is only the fourth time we've met and, not wishing to overuse the cliché, it's like I've known you for years, she said. So, It's a bit more complicated, Andiara, because, yes, there is somebody, I lived with somebody, We lived together for a few good years and then we separated, It's just that at the end of last year we ran into each other and ended up hooking up again, I said. You fucked, she said. Yes, we fucked, I said. After you'd been separated for how long, she asked. Fifteen years, I replied. Hooking up with her messed with your head, she said. Yeah, I said. Oh pal, this is quite the situation you've got yourself into, she said. And so this is what I'm like now, with this crazy end-of-the-party feeling, like nothing's really worth it, Feeling like life, this life of mine, looking at it in perspective, is much less than I'd imagined, I said. A classic turning-fifty crisis, a classic drop in the body's testosterone level, Nothing that can't be resolved in the blink of an eye, she said, and I saw she too was drunk. You're terrible, I said. You're going to have to choose, Either I'm terrible or I'm incredible, she said, And I can tell you now, I'd rather be terrible, I spend almost all my energy trying to be incredible in the day-to-day stuff with the Prosecution Service, she concluded. Terrible, I emphasised. She got up from her chair and, across the table, gave me a long kiss on my forehead. At tomorrow's dinner you'll tell me who this person is, she said, she sat back down and asked for the bill, the bill that it was my turn to pay.

At the third dinner, the one the following night, at the Arab Emporium in 215-South, no sooner had we settled at the table than she notified me that she'd changed her mind, that she no longer wanted to know why a handsome, healthy guy like me was in such a strange mood, that what she could do was respect me and continue to be available to meet me at night for us to do fun things, without fucking, like two friends who are attracted to each other can always do. Two new friends who have managed to find the secret code to making Brasília less dull than it was before, I said. And she agreed. We went out five more times, twice to the movies, three times for dinner. At one of them we ended up at the hotel where she was staying, and we fucked, and it was good.

The commission was on its fifth day of meetings, the following day was going to be the sixth gathering of the group. Being with Andiara was getting better and better. That night's dinner, which happened to fall on the night of Brazil's Independence celebrations, would be our seventh overall. We agreed to meet at nine thirty at Tejo in 404-South. She was doing an interview with a federal judge from Fortaleza, a woman who was an authority on the market and social justice, who'd helped found the PSOL party when she lived in Rio Grande do Sul, but who subsequently ended up leaving academic life and political activism to compete for a place on the federal magistracy, and who happened to be passing through Brasília, and things ran late. She arrived at ten, apologising. While she told me excitedly how incredible the judge was, some messages started coming in on my WhatsApp, I ignored them, but when I started to receive them by SMS I checked. I'd had ten phone calls, but I'd managed somehow to mute them all. It was my brother. I didn't waste time listening to the voicemail messages he'd left, I excused myself to Andiara, got up, went out to the restaurant's lobby, called him. Hi, Lourenço, What's up, bro, I said. I'm kind of in a daze here, 'derico, Roberta's been arrested, he said. That caught me by surprise. Roberta, my only brother's only daughter, my niece who was also my goddaughter, who had lost her mother at the age of eight in a car accident, an accident Lourenço refused to talk about. Arrested, How come, I asked. She went to a protest organised by one of those student political militant groups that communicate on WhatsApp, And she went in her little VW Beetle, They picked her up at a temporary police roadblock, they took the car, Look at the WhatsApps I sent you, Look at them now, And I need you to come here, he said. Don't worry, bro, They do arrest students, but they end up letting them go, Prison space is at such a premium during the crisis, they've got no way of keeping students locked up, I said this because it was the best way I could think of to try to calm him down, because I knew that in that second semester of twenty sixteen, yes, university students did get arrested, and yes, they stayed arrested, Have you already found a lawyer, I asked. Yes, Federico, There's already one working to get her out, It's Augusto, the father of one of my basketball players from the club, one of the best lawyers in Porto Alegre, So I'm going to hang up now, Look at the WhatsApp messages

I sent you, Please, he said. My brother would never ask for a favour over the phone if it wasn't serious. I'll hang up here, We'll talk on Whats, he said again and hung up.

I looked at the messages on WhatsApp and they said that, because of the repercussions of a number of protests against the repossession of a public building that had been occupied months earlier by families from the Movement of Homeless Workers, the military police had done a number of blitz checks using roadblocks equipped with heavy weaponry and everything on the main roads out of Porto Alegre's Historic Centre, and Roberta's Beetle got stopped at one of these, the Beetle that was probably already being monitored by the undercover P2 branch, and they made her get out of the car, checked the boot, the engine, the interior, and found Anísio's .32 revolver, news that froze me to the spot, this being the same .32 we'd hidden in the attic of our house on Coronel Vilagran Cabrita in nineteen eighty-four, the revolver that Anísio'd had, and which had only ever been used, with disastrous consequences, by Anísio himself, as Lourenço, when he had got over his reluctance, only got around to telling me the day after we hid it, the story being that Anísio, after we all ran away from the fight outside the Leopoldina Juvenil, decided to go after Rita, a girl from Oscar Pereira who had some kind of uncontrollable power of attraction over him, he tried to hold back but there was just no way, it was some kind of witchcraft, as he put it, she was at a party at the Middle Way Club in Santa Cecília, he managed to get a ride back to his place, changed clothes, took off his docksiders and T-shirt, put on his leather boots, one of his striped short-sleeved shirts, the one he was wearing when he appeared in front of us at Billy's Xis Van, a shirt in the style of that Lúcio Flávio bandit movie, the style Rita liked, and as he'd done on a couple of other occasions, he decided to borrow one of his brother's guns, his brother who was a corporal in the military police, he took it to impress the girl, and he headed off on his motorbike to the Middle Way, and there he found Rita, he invited her to go for a ride, she suggested they go to get some chips at Mac Dinho's on the corner of São Luís and Princesa Isabel, one of the most popular places in the city, and then head back to the Middle Way, and when they got to Mac Dinho's, surrounded by the mob of teenagers who swarmed the sidewalks and part of the road while there was a show going on with motorbike wheelies, revving motors, tyre-smoking starts, and races off the traffic lights on Princesa Isabel, and while they were deciding whether they really would stick around to order their fries, which might all end up being a massive flop as the place was too full and they'd have to eat them standing, or just give up and go back to the party at the Middle Way, four of the gremistas who'd been at the trouble outside the Leopoldina Juvenil showed up, and seeing the four of them approaching, even noticing that they seemed unmistakably like a bunch of guys out looking for some other guys, some guys with whom they wanted to settle accounts, Anísio didn't get alarmed, on the contrary, he stayed cool, he didn't give himself away, he was wearing different clothes, he was in another context, he thought he could go unnoticed, but one of the guys spotted Rita, and then this guy recognised Anísio, and that guy told the others, and then the four of them were on top of him, and the one who'd been in a K&K surfer T-shirt, the only one who wasn't in a Grêmio T-shirt, even pulled a knuckleduster out of his pocket, Anísio asked Rita to stay where she was and he ran out and down São Luís towards Ipiranga, then he turned right onto Leopoldo Bier, the guys were a lot bigger than him, with longer legs, and however wild like Wolverine he might have been when it came to fighting, there was nothing he could do, halfway down the block he stopped, turned round, pulled out the gun, fired up in the air, three of them stopped but the one who was wearing the brass knuckles, the one in the K&K surfer T-shirt, didn't even slow down, Anísio shot him in the chest, and he tumbled down, and gun in hand, aiming at the others, who shrank back, Anísio walked right past the fallen body and past the other three guys, he went as far as the corner with São Luís and, totally disregarding the bystanders who were looking fearfully at that guy holding a gun, kept going as far as his motorbike, put the revolver in his belt, unlocked the handlebars, put on his helmet, started up the bike, drove back to the neighbourhood, back to Partenon, where he met us at Billy's Xis Van with that damn pistol, that gun which belonged to his psycho brother, a seriously fucking violent officer, star of the military police's karate team, who was quite capable of strangling Anísio if he got hold of him, that gun we decided to hide because Anísio, who wasn't about to turn himself in, though he knew the guys from Moinhos de Vento weren't going to just let him get away with it, because Anísio, despite everything, said to Lourenço that hiding the gun was the best thing to do in a situation like that. I froze to the spot, truly. I could have fired off some messages to my brother asking where the fuck he'd hidden the gun that his daughter, aged eighteen, was able to find it and take it to a protest in the centre of the city, I could've asked why, why the hell he hadn't given the gun to me on one of the many times in the intervening years I'd asked him to hand it over so I could try to get rid of it for good, I could've told him don't even think about letting our dad know that Roberta's been arrested, I could've said a whole lot of other things too, but I imagined everything that must have been going through his head at that moment and, telling myself that I would take all the responsibility for the provenance of that gun, because getting arrested for carrying an unlicensed firearm was no joke, I managed to hold back and texted him only that I'd be on the first flight to Porto Alegre in the morning.

I went back to Andiara. Her face was glowing, she wanted to tell me the things the judge had said, she wanted to know how my visit to the University of Brasília that morning had gone when I'd been to meet a group of students who had questions about the workings of our commission, students who were a part of a national collective that, even though they themselves continued to defend the quota system, were committed to damping down the conflicts between students for and against quotas, Andiara wanted to talk about what our strategy for the following day's meeting of the commission was going to be. I couldn't talk about the gun, the gun that hadn't been on my list of concerns for a long time now, and I didn't want to talk about Roberta's imprisonment. All right, Federico, she asked. All right, I replied, It's just I'm going to have to go to Porto Alegre early tomorrow, And before you ask, I can tell you it's nothing serious, It's just something that requires my presence, I said. My niece's situation was certainly serious, but I wasn't a lawyer, I was the uncle who was going to shoulder all the blame about the provenance of the gun or whatever, because I was aware of it having been my hot-headedness that, directly or indirectly, had led Anísio to twice pull the trigger. The responsibility was mine, whatever Lourenço said. Admitting it to myself, knowing that the .32 was back in our lives, that the responsibility was mine alone, calmed me, centred me instantly. Yes, my niece's situation was serious, but it was only one part of a whole hellish landscape I could not erase, out of an excess of guilt, out of weakness, a vast landscape in which the gun was only a tiny detail, a speck, but a piece of hell nonetheless, a hell feeding parasitically upon the consciences of all the Federicos I'd been, in turn, over more than thirty years, a hell that made all the other conceivable hells of daily life seem like the merest sparks in an everyday reality that my own way of seeing, my own way of reading life, refused to accept, a reality hemmed in on all sides by the catastrophe that people call racism, by the psychic devastation it causes, whatever other people might say to try to convince me it wasn't as bad as all that, that the hatred and disgust directed at blacks had more or less died away, that things had been so much worse in the past, yes, my niece's situation was serious, but I needed to tell myself that Porto Alegre and the sudden and complete return of the nightmare I had never really forgotten could wait, I wouldn't be jeopardising anything by staying with Andiara in that res-taurant for a little longer, I could go deal with airline tickets and everything else after dinner. I asked if we were drinking wine, Andiara said she wasn't sure, that she'd had a glass of sparkling wine with the judge, that maybe it was best not to mix and to stay on the sparkling.

After almost an hour of conversation, Andiara decided once and for all to break the siege of the perennial equilibrium that was one of her most striking features. You know, Federico, You could at least tell me, explain to me, what it is that makes you want to be with me but not to get involved with me, she asked. It's just me, Andiara, I'm just tired is all, I said. Tired, she asked. Yeah, a tiredness that started last year, That just showed up in a very ordinary situation, I said. Can you tell me, she asked. Sure, I said, So I was in a taxi, I'd left my parents' house, I was headed for the airport down in Porto Alegre, and out of nowhere, Well, I mean, so I do think it was a bit because my dad, who's a really active guy for eighty-five, gave me a pretty hard time when I went by their house to say goodbye to them, He was really pushing me, kind of pressuring me, saying I should go into politics, I should join a party, I should campaign, get elected, try to be a political leader, and not just go on treading water endlessly, the way supporting players do, the way that I as a supporting player was doing, On the back seat of that cab I just went into this deep mental tunnel, I asked myself if I really had the stomach to face a term in parliament, I started going back over all the things I still imagined I'd do with my life, all the possible paths I could take, and I couldn't see myself happy or fulfilled in any of them, None of them seemed really persuasive enough to justify, oh I don't know, to justify my existence, my enthu-siasm, to justify the expenditure of my reserves of vital energy, I said. It happens, Federico, sometimes we're anxious and don't even realise it, Our brain shoots off, flooding us with dozens of questions, images and expectations that we can't just deal with in a single second, she said. I'm an anxious person, Andiara, You know, when I was twenty I was diagnosed as suffering from anxiety, And I can spot the signs when an anxiety attack is on its way, After a few years of therapy, I learned to switch off the machinery, The anxiety still shows up but I don't allow it to develop into anything, No, that sudden mental wobble in the taxi wasn't anxiety, It really wasn't, It was just me realising I'd discarded an intolerable quantity of things that had been important to me over the course of the journey, the great voyage, And among those important things, which I can count on the fingers of my hands, there was, and is, as a part of most of them, always the same one person, a person who'd been important to me at the end of my adolescence, at the start of adulthood and still to this day, And her, that person, the one I clung to whenever I realised I was losing my balance, that person was the one I blamed whenever I needed to find somebody who really loved me that I could blame, and that person I devoted myself to like I've never managed to devote myself to anyone else again, To her, And her happiness, Her certainty, And even her faults, I said, slightly awkward, slightly ashamed. What's her name, Andiara asked, and I could see in her face that this question wasn't going to be her last. Bárbara, I said. And she works with black kids too, she asked. In a way, She's a psychologist with experience in the clinical care of activists, of militants in popular movements, the ones who throw themselves in head first, who think about other people before themselves, who fight for more social justice in this sham country of ours, and who, because they don't respect certain boundaries or because they even aren't aware of those boundaries, because they get caught up in some extraordinary situation or other or are just unlucky, wind up traumatised, It's very common, you know, this business of being an activist, being a militant walking around with some serious trauma, I said. I know, there's a lot of people like that in my life up in the north, she said. Yeah, And it's a long list, She sees people fighting against police violence in the favelas, people fighting to reduce domestic violence, fighting against murders committed in the countryside on the orders of some farmowner, some mayor, some governor, people who support indigenous leadership, you know, the sorts of people who engage in any kind of struggle against any kind of oppression, people who expose themselves like that aren't always able to maintain their emotional equilibrium, their mental health, And so on, I said. You changed completely when you started talking about her, Andiara observed. We went out in high school, I said, Then she dumped me for some guy, an older guy who showed her stuff that I, a poor little nobody who trailed after other people who were more enlightened, even while fancying himself better than any of them, could never have shown her. Later, years later, we met up again, and she helped me to slightly reduce the anger I have inside me, an anger that makes my anxiety look like nothing, We started going out again and ended up living together, kind of like married, Well I mean, married, I said. Until you separated, she said. We stayed together for six years, that was when I became this jack-of-all-trades on behalf of the country's black youth that I still am today, I said. Six years, a good while, Andiara observed. Yeah, We stayed together till one day I wavered, I said. And wavering means what exactly, Andiara asked. It means a lot of things, it means making choices that, I'd say, maybe aren't the most reliable choices when you're trying to fulfil a promise, the promise to try to be happy alongside someone who really needs you to be happy, choices that brought back the noise, the anger that not only eats away at my happiness but makes me need to tear up the happiness of the person closest to me, choices that made me keep having those feelings till I finally blew up. I'm not sure I follow, she said, and gestured to the waiter. Are you going to ask for another bottle of sparkling, I asked. Exactly, my friend, she said. I won't be joining you, I warned her. She looked at me and winked. The waiter came over. Another sparkling wine, And a mineral water, and she waited for him to leave and then said, I'd like to stay with you a little longer, Would that be OK, she asked, You have your water and I'll drink enough to prevent my superego from slapping me out of bed in the morning to show up at our commission meeting, You can put that down on my annual solidarity quota, You're going to miss it so I'll miss it too, A pure gesture of solidarity with a colleague, she joked. Where shall we go then, I asked. We're going on a journey to Federico's-Regrets Station, and she just went on looking at me. I do think there's a bit of regret, yeah, But what really weighs me down is the feeling that what I'm tired of is myself, that I'm tired of the life I've had, of what I've tried to do and failed, of my insignificance, an insignificance I've always tried and failed to escape, I explained. Tiredness with yourself, Makes sense, she said, And flirting, Falling in love, Being in a relationship,

Are they also in this bundle of tiredness, she asked. I can't flirt any more, Andiara, Not now, Though I can get interested in somebody who's worth it, But when it involves some emotional connection, it's just that new situations, and I don't want to be crude, but everything feels like just more of the same, I said. But there are so many cool people in the world, and she raised her index finger. There are, Andiara, Getting at cool people is easy, Getting away from them, when I see that I'm failing to give anything back, again and again, that's what keeps getting harder, more meaningless, more painful, I said. The waiter brought the sparkling wine and the water, he filled Andiara's wine glass and my tumbler. You know, Brasília's a port, It doesn't have boats, but it's a port, People shouldn't live in ports, Ports are always unstable places, dangerous ones, very dangerous, she said, looking drunkenly at her glass. Maybe you're right, I said. How long has it been since you last saw Bárbara, she asked. Last time she and I met was December eighth last year, a week after that time we hooked up, At a party at a friend's place, She was with the guy who's now her boyfriend-husband, I was kind of drunk, And I proposed to her, I said. In front of her boyfriend, she asked. No, Of course not, I'm not that kind of idiot. And she never talked to you again after that, she said. I can see you've been doing some research into my life, Andiara, I said, and she laughed, shook her head and also waggled her index finger no. Tell me more, Federico, still smiling. I don't think so, Andiara, I'll talk about Bárbara some other time, I said. She's not the reason you're going to Porto Alegre then, Andiara said. No, I'm not going to Porto Alegre because of her, I'm going to Porto Alegre to help my brother, He's got a really serious problem that needs solving, a problem that's also partly my problem, He's the kind of guy who doesn't ask for help, but this time he did, And I've got to help him, I said. I'm sorry, she said. Why, I asked. Because I pushed it, Because I pushed it willingly, willingly and with just a hint of cruelty, And you were a gentleman, So I promise not to bring up the Bárbara-In-Your-Life thread again, she picked up my glass of water, took three sips, Your brother's important to you, It was lovely hearing you, those times you've talked to me about him, The sense I get is he's very lucky to have an older brother who drops everything when he calls, It's lovely to see two brothers who get along, It's so depressing seeing brothers becoming estranged, Brothers who get estranged, who hate each other, it's so telenovela tune in at nine, she said. We've had our estrangements, I said, and checked the time. It was already gone one in the morning, but I couldn't say let's go, not before she gave some indication that she was ready to go, I picked up the bottle of sparkling wine, poured her a glass and one for myself. You know, I'm an older sister, I take care of my three siblings the way you must take care of yours, but I don't think I can understand them the way you understand yours, she said. You're mistaken, I said, I may try to understand the world around my brother, That's a fact, But the world around Lourenço will never be the same as mine. Yes, she said. I'm going to tell you a story, something I've never told anyone, Do you want to hear it, Andiara, I asked. Please, and for the first time she checked her watch, I'm listening, And then we'll go, You're travelling tomorrow, I don't want to be responsible for you missing your flight, And you haven't even bought your ticket yet, crazy man, she said. In twenty twelve,

I spent two weeks in Porto Alegre, I said, And there was this one night Lourenço invited me to go to a show by Graforreia Xilarmônica, a band from down there in the south, I'm a big fan of theirs, The show was in a place called Opinion, We met two of his friends there, twin brothers, guys from Novo Hamburgo, a city that's right next to Porto Alegre. I know Novo Hamburgo, Andiara said. Well then, these were two guys who'd played ball with my brother back when he was in the juniors, He got out his phone and asked me to take a photo. When I saw the flash was on, I turned it off, took the picture. Lourenço asked me to take another with flash. I chose a new angle and without activating the flash took another two photos, I said photos using flash were for amateurs, and I handed back his phone. The brothers, who'd only just arrived, went off to buy a few beer tokens. Lourenço checked the photos and said to me, You always insist on not using the flash, 'derico, But you got to use it with me, otherwise when it's kind of dark like now I don't show up properly. He said this with a biting calm, and I nodded, I demonstrated that I'd understood, At the beginning of the show, I said I'd go get us a couple of beers, I left the dance floor, but I didn't go to the bar, I went to the bathroom, went into one of the cubicles, closed the door and cried, I cried like I hadn't cried in ages, Do you see, I asked, I'm so proud and so full of myself about being the older brother, being the protector, But, fuck, it took me years, decades to notice that one detail that was so obvious and so important to him, Just try to imagine the rest, I said. Andiara got up from her chair, walked around the table, made me get up and hugged me, and said it was time for us to go.

There are eleven of us in the trapezium-shaped enclosure on John Paul I Square, right by Santa Teresinha Street, in the Santana neighbourhood, some of us perched on the backs of the benches, some sitting down, some stretched out on the grass. Just one more group of so many groups that are formed, by affinity, among the first-year students at the Federal University of Rio Grande do Sul. Making the most of the fact that it's a Friday evening, talking about music and movies, and later theatre and books, parties and sex. Quiti, aged eighteen, a Library Sciences student, the daughter of a teacher in the state school system and a manager at the Federal Savings Bank, is reading out loud from the journalist Pepe Escobar's article on *Purple Rain*, Prince's sixth album, in a two-day-old copy of *Folha de São Paulo* that Antônio, aged eighteen, a law student, the son of a lawyer and a state judge, picked up from the student union hub of the law faculty. It says in the article that Prince is a young black Dionysus who is planning to subvert normative social relations through an explosion of unbridled libido via his work as a pop artist, going on to say that the song 'Let's Go Crazy' is a synthesis of his pagan thought, preaching salvation through partying, an erotic ceremony able to demolish reason, that the song

'Purple Rain' is like a meeting between Lennon and Hendrix at a table in a bar to talk about emotional vulnerabilities and to lament a lost love, that the album is closely related to a movement called electrobeat, which is the sound of the big cities, forged from the mutant crack cocaine of drum machines like the LinnDrum and the Oberheim DMX, led by blacks and Puerto Ricans in the Bronx, Algerians and Africans in Paris, the children of foreign workers in Berlin, blacks living off social security in north London, kids from the São Paulo suburbs. As Quiti reads she gives these little giggles that make the rest of us laugh too. Residents of the Vila Planetário community walk past us, registering our ease, our freedom. I suspect that none of these new friends of mine notice even one of those passers-by, those very low-paid people returning home tired from work. Talking about Prince's new album and about the things happening in the world, things that only we can possibly know about, we who are so young and secure in our intelligence and have access to newspapers and magazines that report on what's new and innovative, this the most important thing of all. It's not their fault, not my new friends' fault, it's not their problem that I can't completely get my head out of the place I've come from, that I can't get rid of the way of seeing things that I learned back home, that I can't look at them, despite my having been blessed with almost all the same opportunities as them, despite my having light skin like them, I just can't look at them without seeing a band of well-off little white kids who come from neighbourhoods that have nothing in common with Partenon, and that's even though my own Partenon of recent years has nothing in common with the Partenon of a person who didn't have the family support I've had. Cavalheiro, aged nineteen, a social sciences student, the son of university history professors, his mother at Unisinos and his father at UFRGS, starts reading the list of movies showing in São Paulo this week: *Gorky Park, Beat Street, Sudden Impact, The Outsiders, Indiana Jones and the Temple of Doom, Memórias do Cárcere, Quilombo, Jango, Splash, Os Trapalhões e o Mágico de Oróz*. Plato, aged seventeen, a history student, son of a widowed psychologist, says that only *Beat Street* and *Os Trapalhões* appeal. Carlo, aged nineteen, a history student, son of the general manager of the João Pessoa Mall and the manager of Casa Masson on the Rua da Praia, says Plato doesn't understand anything, the movie with the mermaid is the only bit of proper cinema on that list. Quiti says she's spending her money on *The Outsiders*, she's not going to pass up a Coppola movie with a cast that includes Patrick Swayze, beautiful Diane Lane, that Rob Lowe who's so cute, Emilio Estevez, C. Thomas Howell and Tom Cruise. Everybody laughs. Claudia, aged seventeen, a journalism student, the daughter of surgeons, the most well-born kid present, picks up the Friday edition of the *Folha de São Paulo* that she just bought at the round news stand in Alfândega Square in the city centre before coming to meet us, pulls out an article by Décio Pignatari to read to us. She starts, but she doesn't have Quiti's charisma. Some people start to drift away as she reads. She's sitting on the grass as she reads, and when she reaches the end of the article, unwilling to renounce our attention, which is hers by right, she gets to her feet and starts up again. I don't believe it is too optimistic a view, she reads, to conclude that the military's cynical control of the Brazilian people these past two decades must

92

surely be having some kind of positive effect, We are ceasing to be optimists, An optimistic people is an underdeveloped people, Pessimism is what is needed, Pessimism doesn't allow itself to be conned, it learns to identify the true value and quality of things and people, You need only give a little smile and power sticks its hand in your pocket, In today's Brazil only the military are free, Perhaps that's why they only talk about the green-and-yellow in the flag, which actually they've been doing since the days of our amusing proclamation of the Republic, amusing precisely because it never gets to be anything more than a proclamation, They've stolen the blue of the sky and the blue of the flag, They just kept the stars, I dunno, maybe because blue symbolises freedom, At least it does on the French flag, she reads with dramatic weight. Four officers from the military police pass us on horseback, probably coming from Vila Planetário headed towards Parque da Redenção. They don't approach us. It's their stop-and-frisk time, the time for taking a close look at who's hanging out with whom, what they're saying, what they're doing. Carlo says Claudia couldn't have timed it better, she spoke of the devil and the devil appeared. Plato says he can't bear going through any more hassle from those morons on Independência, on Osvaldo Aranha, on Venâncio Aires, on José do Patrocínio. Cikuta, aged seventeen, a history student, the daughter of the owners of the most famous Portuguese restaurant in the city, says she attended a discussion between Décio Pignatari and Paulo Leminski in the university auditorium last year, that she couldn't tell which of the two was the most insane, which the biggest genius. Raquel, aged seventeen, a social sciences student, daughter of a dentist father and a mother in advertising, says she was there too, that it had been an event in one of those UniTeatro programmes. Cikuta confirms this. Confirming each other's statements, giving off a libidinous intellectual complicity, is a big part of our tacit agreement of guaranteed satisfaction. Quiti, who has taken the newspaper from Claudia, now starts reading extracts from the *Ilustrada* cover interview that Jorge Mautner gave to the journalist Ruy Castro. Quiti doesn't need to make the least effort when she reads, everybody just listens. Are you the last living existentialist, asks Ruy Castro, I must be, I follow the teachings of my Lord Jesus Christ who said that the last would be first, replies Mautner, What would you say to those who suspect this whole chaos business isn't disorder so much as deception, asks Ruy Castro, Well that's certainly a part of it, isn't it, replies Mautner, What is this chaos party going to be like, asks Ruy Castro, Mautner replies that it'll be a mixture of a political party, a supra-partisan one, and an ecumenical religion, whose main temple will be in São Paulo, it will have its own anthems, cells, fees, basically whatever you'd expect from a big club, Quiti reads. Everybody laughs. Then there's this bit that's cool too, Quiti goes on, Ruy asks, Why do you, as an out homosexual, not share this message of homosexuality in your lyrics, and Mautner replies, Well I do in some, like in the lyrics of 'I Am a Vampire', but it just so happens that homosexuality isn't my main concern, Freud said all humans are bisexual, Well I say human beings are pansexual and can have sex with anything, even a table or a chair. To which Ruy says Wow, and asks whether it's strange that, given that sex is so important, political parties never refer to it in their platforms, And Mautner replies, Well, if president-to-be

Tancredo Neves invites me to take on a post in his cabinet, I'll say I think it's important to talk about everything, Have you ever stopped to think about how spiritually profound our football has become, To which Ruy asks, Then again, isn't all this a bit too fluid and ethereal, And Mautner replies, But that's the philosophy of chaos, Quiti reads. I agree that humanity's bisexual, says Raquel. I'm very bisexual, says Quiti. Me too, says Carlo. I'm just non-practising, says Quiti. Everybody laughs. Mautner's my guru, says Plato. The daylight is starting to fade. Anyone want to catch a movie later, asks Carlo. I'm always up for a movie, says Antônio. Federico, you up for that, asks Carlo. I've got other plans, I reply. Federico's always got other plans, says Claudia. Federico's a real mystery man, says Antônio. I'm going to a party at the Leopoldina Juvenil with my brother and some friends, No big deal, I say. I'd be up for going to the movies, says Claudia, but only if it's to see *Memórias do Cárcere*, It's playing at the Coral, And the Coral's right by my apartment, and she laughs. That title, *Prison Memoirs*, it reminds me of my entrance exams, says Cikuta, I want to get a long way from those exams, and she pulls one of her faces. I'm in, says Carlo, Ten o'clock screening, right, he asks. Right, says Claudia. I don't know, says Antônio, The movie I want to see, I mean out of the domestic ones, is *Quilombo*, it's the midnight screening at the ABC, which is opposite *my* apartment, and he gives Claudia's shoulder a little shove. Today they've got Bergman's *The Magic Flute* at the Goethe Institut at nine, Quiti says, I'm just telling you, I'm not going, Like this enigmatic little cutie here, and she hugs me, I've got other plans, My secret lover is coming round to mine so we can listen to the latest from Yellow Magic

Orchestra, which he got bootlegged from Buenos Aires, she says. Cikuta talks about going to the Blue Angel to watch her cousin, who's a musician with the Porto Alegre Symphony, playing piano, she says he starts playing at eight thirty. Claudia asks if the bar on Fernandes Vieira is totally bisexual. Cikuta nods. Some guys who look like construction workers, possibly from Vila Planetário, walk past talking loudly about the Olympics. And I realise none of my new friends have even brought up the topic of the Olympics. Cavalheiro steers the conversation to a new subject, and after him somebody adds another subject still. We all stay in the square until it's dark.

When the voice of the lawyer hired to defend Roberta, broadcast via Bluetooth through the speakers in my brother's Renault Duster, suggested, as we travelled from the airport towards the centre of the city, that we meet him at the Burger King on Ipiranga because it was the easiest place to find, to park, it had good air conditioning and the perfect atmosphere, because it was swarming with shouty teenagers, which was a guarantee that nobody would hear our conversation, besides being really close to the Police Headquarters jail, he left us in no doubt that we had a long afternoon ahead of us. The officer in charge of the case had found nothing in his investigation to suggest that the charges were meritless, nor did he want to set bail, among the justifications cited being the fact that the .32 was registered as belonging to the military police, which fact suggested to him that it might be best to leave it to the presiding judge to decide how to proceed when he received the official notice conveying the legal basis of the arrest in flagrante, a notice that had been sent by the city's Central Courthouse first thing that morning. Augusto said it could have been worse, but it wasn't a simple case, there were aggravating circumstances, some of them milder, others more serious, to be taken into account, aggravating circumstances that the lawyer would enumerate and detail when we met shortly at the Burger King.

Before unwrapping his Whopper, the same burger Lourenço and I had ordered, Augusto made a point of telling me what a brave girl Roberta was, she knew how to keep calm, not to make so much as a peep in front of the police until he, her appointed lawyer, arrived at the Police Headquarters cells, he said she had been brilliant during the detainee's preliminary questioning, stating that she'd found the revolver in one of the Alfândega Square flower beds while she was running away from the stun grenades, the tear gas, the rubber bullets that the military police were firing into the groups of protesters, that she had remained calm all the while and that she was convincing when she said that she'd only picked the gun up on impulse and, on impulse, put it into her rucksack.

While he ate his fries and his burger and gave us the odds of the judge granting habeas corpus, granting release or setting bail, I, who still hadn't unwrapped my burger and was sitting next to one of Burger King's enormous front windows, alternated glances between this performance by a practitioner of the Law in front of clients nervous about his predictions, on my right, and the iron and glass entrance to the Second Police Precinct jail, on my extreme left, on the other side of the Dilúvio canal, a little over a hundred metres in a straight line from where we were, the most emblematic feature of the northern façade of the Police Headquarters building, where the military police had taken Roberta the previous night and where she was still being detained, which was a piece of luck, actually, given that after the physical examination at the Institute of Forensic Medicine and the docketing of the case she could easily have been taken to the women's prison, but, thanks to Augusto the lawyer's intervention, everything seemed to suggest, she wasn't. Between those two reference points, lawyer and prison, stood the João Pessoa bridge, the only bridge in the world to have imperial palms growing right out of the structure itself, eight vast specimens, direct descendants of the palms in the Botanical Gardens in Rio de Janeiro, specimens planted accidentally by the municipal workers at the start of the nineteen forties, or so it said in the annals of the Porto Alegre town hall, and yet, thanks to the peculiarity of their roots, designed to look for water in the desert ground of California, in the United States, where they originated, unable to do real harm to the bridge's concrete structure, still bravely resisting the weather after more than seven decades, not least the strong winds channelled along the Dilúvio, roots that would outlive, no doubt, that Burger King where we were sitting, would outlive me, my brother and our lawyer, who at that moment, after concluding his predictions about habeas corpus, release, bail, remarked that another thing weighing very much in our favour was the fact that the Federal Supreme Court had years ago decreed the unconstitutionality of the articles of the Disarmament Law that banned bail for cases of illegally carrying firearms deemed to be of permitted use.

The explanations and conjectures came in big chunks, with no change in rhythm, it was almost hypnotic the way the lawyer moved on to new issues and the arguments deriving from each. And it was at the end of the explanations and conjectures, when he had already done away with his Whopper and fries, that he said he had one extra piece of information to relate, it might turn out to be nothing but still couldn't be dismissed out of hand. He revealed that he had heard, late that morning, in the Police Headquarters itself, that some high-ranking somebody-or-other was raising the possibility of Roberta's being charged under the antiterrorism law, a law that had come into effect that same year, twenty sixteen. Now I completely stopped paying attention to what was happening outside the window and focused on what the lawyer was saying. Lourenço asked who this high-ranking person was. Augusto said he didn't know, but he was going to start trying to track down the information that very afternoon. Without hiding my annoyance that he, one of the best lawyers in Porto Alegre, should have waited till that moment to share such a serious piece of information, I counted to ten and then asked what the factual basis would be for an accusation of that kind. He explained that two other cars had been picked up by the police at temporary roadblocks around the city's Historic Centre, he said that in one of them, a Volkswagen Saveiro, in the possession of an Agronomy student, there were products in the trunk containing a high percentage of ammonium nitrate, a substance that can be used in the production of explosives, and in the other, a Fiat Uno belonging to a Law student, there were pamphlets filled with hateful propaganda and incitements to violence against the state governor, though it would be very difficult, but not impossible, for the cops to allege that the three of them were in cahoots in some kind of terrorist cell. Lourenço asked whether the problem was no longer the fact of her being caught carrying a gun but carrying a gun for terrorist purposes. Augusto said terrorists would never go around with a gun that couldn't be used like that revolver, which was loaded with old bullets that would have never been usable, and given his previous remarks about his client's alleged possession of the .32, in one of his chunks of explanations and conjectures, he stressed that it counted greatly in our favour that the four bullets found in the cylinder of the revolver, even though they looked fine, with their casings in good condition, were completely useless, since both the projectiles and primer were rusty, adding that even the best bullets on the market, bullets of the very highest quality, unlike the bullets from the confiscated gun, didn't have a functional life exceeding ten years, and that the lack of any records as to the provenance of the weapon in the military police's files also counted in our favour, meaning some documentation about which of the force's officers the gun was intended for, and Augusto went on to remark that if such a document existed, well, he'd be worried, but just knowing the firearm had been manufactured in nineteen eighty-two and that it was acquired by the government of Rio Grande do Sul for use by the police that same year wasn't much for them to go on, no, it didn't amount to much, not much at all, there were no records identifying who'd lost the gun or how they'd lost it, and consequently this made the establishing of any immediate and solid link to Roberta impracticable. I asked whether in that case the terrorism angle was a theory that they would have to abandon, but the lawyer stared me down then and said that even with it being very low in probability it was a threat we shouldn't minimise, let alone discard. Trying not to get myself worked up for nothing, as I knew the implications of Brazilian antiterrorism law, I changed the subject, changed it to something more immediate, asking if I could talk to Roberta, if there was any way of my getting into the Police Headquarters lock-up to talk to her. This only made Augusto suspicious, he asked what my niece would gain by speaking to me, he said I'd probably just get her confused and even, who knows, maybe even make it harder for her to keep her story straight, the version in which she'd found the gun while fleeing political repression, and he said there was a good chance of the judge who was considering the petitions for release or for granting bail asking to hear from her at the detention hearing, and Augusto, experienced lawyer that he was, didn't want to take any chances. I said I was sure I could calm her down, I said I wouldn't tell her that I'd decided to admit that the gun was mine in the event of things getting out of control, as I'd already informed my brother as soon as we got into his van in the airport car park, and I said that he, who was only meeting me in person for the first time now, couldn't know and couldn't understand, but I felt responsible for her having exposed herself so badly. The lawyer asked us to give him a minute, got up, went to the soft-drink machine, filled a glass with ice, returned to the table, opened his briefcase and took out a can of Red Bull Sugarfree, opened it, poured it into the glass, swirled it around for the cold of the ice to take to the drink, said he was sure he could figure out a way to fix it, said that I was known in the city, that everybody knew about my work with disadvantaged young people, that it would depend on which officer was on duty at that moment. Lourenço asked whether the fact of her being the granddaughter of a well-known officer of the gaúcho civil police would make any difference. The lawyer replied that a surname always carried some weight, that he had used our father's name when he'd talked to the duty officer the previous night, that the police was one big family, that whichever officer was on duty would certainly take the relationship into account, especially if he were one of the older ones, and then he drank the energy drink he'd poured into his cup all the way down.

The duty officer gave us fifteen minutes with Roberta. Augusto stayed in the room with us, listening through his earbuds to podcasts about recent case-law decisions that, he said, he usually downloaded to get himself up to date while sitting in Porto Alegre's increasingly gridlocked, chaotic traffic. I sat at a table opposite Roberta. She said nothing, just watched me. The look in her eyes was different from how I remembered it, her face now carried the same expression I'd seen on a lot of the teenagers I worked with. How're you doing, Beta, I asked. I'm good, I'm solid, Federico, she said. That's great, I said. You didn't need to come down from Brasília just because of me, You didn't need to leave your job with the new government, she said. I'm not working for the new government, I'm not a part of the new government, I said. That's not what I read on the internet, she said. I'm working to prevent this quota commission from going down a path it shouldn't, There's a lot of people wanting to put an end to racial quotas for students, I explained. Whatever, she said, and she shrugged, and it was the first time I'd ever felt any kind of aggression from her, leaving me kind of unsure how to react one moment to the next. I'm here, Beta, I said, and I'll be staying here until you're released, till I know you're OK, and I put my right arm on the table, I reached out my hand to her and she put her left arm out and took it. I noticed the tattoo on the inside of her forearm, a boy, a schoolboy judging by his clothes, holding a slingshot with the rubber band stretched to the limit, looking up, ready to fire. You can talk to me, I said, taking my eyes off the tattoo. She shook her head, but I insisted, You can talk. She let a few seconds go by and then out it came. It was really cold last night here in Porto Alegre, The military police didn't honour the agreement, They didn't care about the families in the building, she said sadly, Where were those mothers going to go, those children, she asked, It's totally ridiculous, And my guys knew something like that was going to happen, Which is why we went to show some support, to protest, she said. But you decided to arm yourself, I whispered. She brought her face close to mine. What would you do in my place, she asked. I didn't answer. You want to know, I've been like this since Mari, a friend of mine, a girl I love, took a rubber bullet from the police last month right in her eye, It was at a demo about the government's stupid fucking plan to reform high school education, which is thanks to that same son of a bitch government you're working for, and she let go of my hand, Her eye was lacerated, She's lost sight in it forever, Can you imagine what that's like, The worst part is she only went to the demo because I insisted, She stayed right beside me when I decided to stand on the front line and face up to the police, And I saw it all, I saw the guy who shot her, It was a soldier, a guy who gets trained for this kind of thing, who gets orders like Only shoot at their legs, at the protesters' legs, and never when you're less than twenty metres from your target, Which is already fucking ludicrous, None of it happened, none of those rules were respected, The asshole shot at her from right up close and at the height of the protesters' heads, And Mari, who isn't even the kind of person who goes to protests, lost her eye, A quiet, lovely girl, from a poor family over in Vila Tarumã, Fucking hell, A girl who really struggled, So determined, and who's now facing an even harder life, Roberta said, unburdening herself to me. I can't imagine, I said. And yesterday, Yesterday, Something in my head kept telling me that if they used rubber bullets against those mothers and those children, I would shoot back, whatever it cost me, I would shoot back, she whispered. And right then on the night of the September seventh celebrations, and I stopped myself. Right, Federico, the day we celebrate our country's fucking independence, What sort of judge would authorise an eviction late at night and on a holiday just to make sure not to inconvenience all the drivers who'd be there any other day, just to keep the city running smoothly, and she looked at me with tears in her eyes, Did you know that's what the judge's argument was, that was the shitty argument this asshole used, she asked. I didn't, I replied. We sat in silence a few seconds, then I said, I'm staying in Porto Alegre till you get out, Beta, We're optimistic, waiting for the judge to decide about granting release, though I chose not to mention bail, And I'm sure everything's going to work out, I said. I just wish I'd had the opportunity and the nerve to shoot at least say three of those cowards, starting with that fucker of a captain who was in command, But I didn't, When they started hitting us I ran off, chickening out, shitting myself like everyone else, she said. It's OK, It's over now, I said, Please, Don't keep thinking about what's already past, I insisted. I can't, That's what I'm like, she said. I know we haven't been close these last few years, I said, I know I haven't been there for your dad, but I'm here now and I'm going to stay here for a few days. She looked right at me and kept looking right at me. And what was in her eyes was no longer chaos, it was something bigger, more dangerous, the most dangerous weapon of all: fear.

Lourenço and I hung around outside the Police Headquarters jail until eight at night. My brother, who remained totally calm until a bit after six, then started to fret, and at seven thirty, after the lawyer called us from the Central Courthouse, saying that the judge wasn't going to decide what to do with Roberta till the following day, he said, devastated, that he was going to try and find out who the duty captain was then and there and tell him the gun was his. I held his arm and for the nth time that day said if anyone was going to do something like that, if anyone was going to take responsibility it would be me, if he did something stupid like say the gun came from him, right in front of a cop then I was going to say the same thing in front of the same cop and we, losers that we were, would thereby ruin the whole strategy put together by the lawyer to get Roberta acquitted when her case went to trial, a trial that was, no doubt, inevitable. He agreed, calmed down, then said that Roberta had always been inspired by my example, that she idolised me, that she thought she had to be politically engaged the way I was and that she romanticised the activist life far too much. I said she had non-conformity in her blood, that she was born with it, that I didn't believe I could have influenced her, being so far away from Porto Alegre. And

106

he said that was the problem, that for somebody who had a niece who read all the history, politics and philosophy books I recommended, watched all the movies I suggested, a niece who adored me, I was too remote from Porto Alegre, I kept myself too distant from her for too long. I said I wasn't really sure what to do to help her, I said maybe it'd be best to find somebody who was a specialist. He said he'd thought about finding a psychologist when her friend lost her eye, he said his daughter had been devastated, but it was only for a few days, that afterwards she promised she'd gotten over it, that she was fine, that the best thing she could do, for her friend and herself, was to be OK, but he said maybe finding the gun had changed her mind on that score, maybe she saw in the possibility of an unforeseen reaction a remedy for all ills. I told him to get those kinds of thoughts out of his head, told him to be careful not to turn the whole business with the gun into a sort of curse. He, who was much more spiritual than I was, replied that curses didn't stick to things, only to people, and he got on his phone to tell the lawyer we were going home soon and that he'd be back at the cells at nine o'clock that night to deliver his daughter another change of clothes and a snack. The lawyer said they could meet at nine o'clock, nine o'clock was good for him, and he asked Lourenço to put him on speakerphone so that I could hear, and then declared that everything would be resolved the following day. I said I hoped he was right and asked if he had any news about the attempt to charge Roberta under the antiterrorism law. He replied that he hadn't heard anything yet, said at some point we'd get the news one way or the other, that it was all part of a game of complex external and internal pressures that weren't always too transparent, a reality beyond his ken, but he said anything of that kind, were it to happen, would happen before the formal charging, and that, in any case, regardless of the view taken by the police, the thing would remain dependent on the Prosecution Service accepting the evidence and the arguments put forward by the investigation and proposing a charge to the criminal judge, who could accept it or not. I thanked him. Finally, idiotically, he said that the whole thing was like fishing, there was a moment for baiting your hook and casting out your line and there was a moment for waiting, just as one would expect an experienced lawyer to act, and he hung up.

I go into the room where the Experimental Psychology II class of the second semester of academic year nineteen eighty-four is being held, I find a desk six rows behind Bárbara's. The students at the back, the only ones who notice my arrival, since the door is at the back of the hall, regard me with indifference. It's the start of the semester, for all they know I could belong there, I could be some new classmate who's only decided to show up at the third class. Like Bárbara, the professor is also sitting with her back to the door, she takes no notice of my arrival. Someone named Ana, whose second name and family names I have no way of knowing, is finishing a presentation. The professor tells her that the points she made were excellent but that she'll wait to make any further comments till all five scheduled presentations are done. The student thanks her, returns to her place. The professor calls another Ana, Ana Rita Santos Carraro, says she has ten minutes to present her work and wishes her good luck. This Ana's presentation is about the behaviour of the accountant in whose office she worked as a secretary until the end of last year, the report is basically about how he behaved when he was working at his desk, how he dealt with incoming phone calls, how he dealt with his clients, how he chatted to his employees, how he used his calculator, how he typed on his IBM electric typewriter when he was in a hurry. The professor repeats the praise she gave the first Ana, says she will provide detailed comments only at the end of the class and calls Bárbara next. I shift position so as not to be so visible to anyone positioned at the blackboard and looking towards the back of the room. Bárbara gets up, walks over to the biggest desk, the professor's desk, puts her notebook and papers on top of it, says good afternoon to her classmates, doesn't see me, doesn't see me because she seems to be focused only on her classmates in the front row, and in any case because she's too near-sighted. The General-President of Brazil, Bárbara reads from the piece of notebook paper in her hands, had a fall from his horse while he was riding in Brasília, Being the robust sixty-something that he is, the General-President of Brazil didn't seem to need any medical attention, But days later he had to be taken to Sarah Kubitschek Hospital with intense pain in his spine and his left leg. In hospital, the General-President of Brazil was immobilised in a plastic orthopaedic corset and kept under observation. The medical team forbade any visitors. Which was a problem, because it's hard enough to keep a president isolated when the country is relatively calm, let alone during an election season, even if the vote that's coming is only for the Electoral College, So the medical team allowed for some exceptions, for example two military ministers were allowed to visit their president, And it was reported in the press that the General-President's spinal injury and enforced isolation only served as a culmination to the crisis of power in relation to the country's governability, With its leader apparently out of circulation, the whole country turned its attention to the vice president of Brazil, a dissident within his own party, And while it was the medical team who ruled out surgical intervention, it was reported in the press that the decision in favour of enforced rest rather than surgery was the General-President of Brazil's decision and his decision alone, not going under the knife being the only way of preventing the vice president of Brazil from ascending to his office, and the General-President of Brazil was gratified to hear that the opposition party candidate had told reporters that the temporary health problem being faced by Mr General-President wasn't going to get in the way of the process of succession in the Electoral College and that the presidential succession itself is on a quite separate path, On Tuesday the General-President of Brazil was released by the medical team, He left the hospital, He was put on total bed rest at the presidential retreat at A Granja do Torto, where he was following all the coverage of the Los Angeles Olympics, The numbness in his leg does annoy the General-President of Brazil, but that's not the thing that annoys him most, What annoys him most is not being able to attend his party's convention to choose its next candidate, and here Bárbara quickly checks her professor's reaction before resuming, The president of Brazil, who at this moment is lying in a special bed for people with spinal problems, is desperate to go to. Bárbara, sorry, the professor interrupts her, I'm going to have to ask you to stop your presentation, You know, And I imagine your classmates have realised, Your work is totally beyond the scope of the assignment, it's not at all what I asked the class to do, You know the idea was to talk about a person you know, a person with whom you have a real relationship, a person who is or was close to you, she stresses, Have you ever been close to our president, Have you had any personal contact with the president of the Republic, she asks. No, Bárbara replies. Then you weren't supposed to write about the president's behaviour, the professor remarks. But my work isn't about the president, it's about me, Bárbara replies, You asked us to do a report about the behaviour of someone we know and want to know more about and I did it about me, About me giving a written report on the behaviour of the president at a critical moment in our nation's recent history. She looks at her classmates and recognises me at last. Even if that's the case, says the professor, it isn't what I asked for, You should have written about the behaviour of somebody who isn't you, says the professor. But you never gave us that restriction, professor, Bárbara retorts. Besides, says the professor, you must be aware that your report wasn't done with the impartiality I required. I disagree, Bárbara replies, looking directly at me, How can I be impartial when I'm reporting on my own behaviour. If you don't have a proper presentation to give us instead of this one, I'm going to ask you to sit down, says the professor. Does that mean I won't be graded for this part of the classwork, Miss Elisabete, asks Bárbara, still looking straight at me and without the slightest embarrassment. It means that, in this piece of work that we've been shown, you'll get a zero, the professor declares, and turns around to see who Bárbara's been staring at. In that case, Bárbara says, returning her attention to the professor, I'll present another report. The professor turns back to face Bárbara. I was worried she was going to ask who I was, but she didn't. Do you have the text there with you, the professor asks. I've got it in my notebook, Bárbara replies. Go right ahead then, But so as not to mess up the programme of our class, and she checks her watch, You'll only have five minutes. No problem, I have three reports about this person ready, I'll just read the shortest, says Bárbara. We're all yours, says the professor. It's raining heavily, Bárbara begins, It's the week before the week when the two boys along with their parents are going to move from their old house at the top of Maria Degolada Hill in Partenon to the new house in a street that's in the same neighbourhood, but which doesn't have a favela nearby, The seventeen-year-old girl who looks after the brothers makes the most of the heavy shower and also the fact of their not having classes that Friday afternoon because the school is being fumigated and will only reopen on Monday, puts rubber boots first on the youngest, then on the older one, She takes the big umbrella, their father's umbrella, and leaves the house with the two of them, They cross the street and walk along the sidewalk opposite till they get to the mouth of the alley, the alley of little wooden shacks that's squeezed between their street, Paulino Azurenha, and the parallel street, Guilherme Alves. They go in, She shows them the kids from the community who, on days when there's a lot of rain, after collecting cardboard boxes from the warehouse close to the Little Kids' House mission, better known as the Maria Degolada house, have fun going down the stream, the gutter, as they call the open-air sewer, that turns into rapids at the ridge of the alley, a kind of water slide fed by the torrent, The youngest asks if he can take a ride on one of those pieces of cardboard, The teenage girl says no, she explains that the three of them are only there to look, to watch, After a few minutes the older

113

boy asks if they can go back home, Then she, this girl who will never look after them again following the family's move to their new house, tells the boys that they should never let the streets and houses to which they're moving erase the memories of where they came from, The older boy says he'll always remember, The younger, holding her hand tight, is giving little jumps and smiling, finding this part of the game highly entertaining, Bárbara finishes reading and, ignoring the professor entirely, takes a few steps towards me, casting onto me her stares of limitless atomic rage. Almost everyone in the class is also looking at me now. I get up, take the envelope from my shirt pocket, I leave it on the desk I've been occupying and make sure that Bárbara, in spite of her myopia, has one hundred per cent noticed that I'm leaving the envelope there for her, I say See you, a see you that I think only those at the back with me can hear, and I withdraw.

I told Lourenço I'd already made my hotel reservation back in Brasília while I was waiting in the airport departure lounge, so I asked if we could quickly stop by the ibis Garibaldi near Farrapos so there wouldn't be any chance of them cancelling it on me, so I could dump my suitcase and my rucksack, and then we'd go to his house to pick up Roberta's things, meet the lawyer at the jail and, who knows, maybe get something for dinner that was healthier than that burger and fries before bringing to a close that day that was so tough for all of us. He said don't take this the wrong way, but he'd prefer it if I just stayed at the hotel, saying that, after going to the police building for the fourth time that day, what he wanted was to go home on his own, have a fennel tea and get some proper sleep, because otherwise he knew he wouldn't be intact, physically and emotionally, for tomorrow. I asked him to at least let me go with him to fetch Roberta's things and then go along with him to the police jail. He thanked me but said for me to stay in the hotel and rest because he was going to need me with all my bloodhound-brother disposition the following day. We went to the hotel, I got out of the car a little annoyed. We said I love you to each other. He said everything was going to work out. I gave a thumbs up. He smiled and pulled away. I went into the ibis, checked in. In the room I turned on the TV, opened my suitcase, took out a pair of socks, a pair of sneakers, swapped them for the ones I was wearing, took a third of a pill for my blood pressure, brushed my teeth, picked up a jacket and left. I got into the taxi that was standing outside the hotel. I told the driver to go to Osvaldo Aranha and, at Osvaldo, to take a left towards the Rio Branco neighbourhood, that after the Tiradentes viaduct I'd show him the way. He asked if I knew the city well. I replied I'd been born and raised in that city. He said I didn't have a gaúcho accent. I said a few years living away had dampened my accent a bit, but that it was still there, solid and strong. He laughed and said that was great, because it was a truly grim thing for a gaúcho to lose his accent.

He pulled in at the apartment block on the corner of Dona Leonor and Professor Álvaro Alvim. I paid the fare, thanked him, got out of the car, went up the steps to the glass door, which was the visitors' entrance to the building, waved at the doorman. He made the universal gesture for Hey use the inter-com that's right there in front of you, dickhead. I pressed the button for the front desk. Good evening, I said. Good evening, he replied. I'd like to talk to Bárbara from three-oh-five, Is she home, I asked, My name's Federico, I'm a friend of hers, I said. Federico what, the doorman asked. Federico Sandman, I replied, and through the glass, I watched as he picked up a telephone handset like something out of a nineteen-nineties intercom switchboard and talked to Bárbara. He unlocked the door. I went in. Miss Bárbara asked you to wait for her in the party room, senhor, Would you come with me please, and he led me away from the lobby towards the door to the party room. He put the key into the lock and looked over his shoulder at me. Nothing like a suspicious doorman to make me even more in the mood for a conversation that, in my head, wasn't going to be at all easy. He opened the door, turned on the lights, said I was to make myself comfortable.

Bárbara took a good ten minutes to come down. Sorry to make you wait, I'm hosting a dinner for a speaker who's come from Chile as a guest of the university department, she said without a hello, without displaying the least annoyance at my having shown up at the front desk of her apartment block without any warning, And sorry not to invite you up, It's just that there are fifteen of us adults and four children up there, There wouldn't be anywhere we could talk privately, she said. I'm the one who should be saying sorry, Showing up here by surprise, I said. But we're past the stage of Bárbara slash Federico being too amazed at any surprises coming from Bárbara slash Federico, and she smiled. I know, I replied. Well then, let's get down to business, What is it you want, Mr Federico Sandman, she said, and laughed. I'm sorry, I said, The doorman, He asked for my full name, and. I know, she said. He does insist on asking for visitors' full names, but he's getting better, He's a good guy, He's just doing his job, she said. Without any more beating about the bush, I told her what had happened to my niece, and also about the impact it seemed to have had on her to witness her friend, perhaps girlfriend, losing an eye because of a rubber bullet fired by a military police officer, and I made some comments about her emotional state, about how I hadn't managed to establish a decent connection with her, and I talked about Lourenço, about the gravity of the whole situation, emphasising that Roberta might well be convicted, that a criminal conviction would ruin her life forever, and I asked what she, Bárbara, the kick-ass psychotherapist, professor at the federal university, with a master's and a doctorate in clinical work with social militants and activists, thought that I, the youth counsellor, but a total loss as far as having a niece caught in flagrante in illegal possession of a firearm, ought to do the next day when I got a second chance to talk to her, whether or not she, Roberta, was free, and how I ought to behave. Lourenço must be feeling such guilt, Bárbara said without thinking. Well, you know what he's like, I said, Always more closed off to me than I'd like him to be, And always so invested in those so-called codes of honour he picked up from the periphery, That business of him promising Anísio he'd look after the gun and then keeping his promise even though there was a real risk of being discovered, that was taking it to absurd lengths, I said. Not to him, to him it makes sense to behave that way, Bárbara said, And I know it's not the cleverest thing in the world, but it makes sense, she concluded. Keeping a gun at home is always a risk, I said. You think he really never imagined his daughter might end up poking around in his things and finding the gun, Bárbara asked. He told me it was somewhere impossible to find, I said. But Roberta's smart, Bárbara said. Yeah, very smart, Except that right now she's not smart at all, she's terrified, You know, However much I try to put a script together in my head for her finding the gun, I can't do it, She'd have to be pretty far from her normal emotional state to be turning the house upside down to the point where she found a pistol that was, in theory, well hidden, What could she have been looking for, I asked. I can't imagine, I can only imagine how shaken up she must be, how upset, how deeply distressed she must be, A girl of eighteen, It all opens up a thousand cavernous unanswered questions, Bárbara said. It's painful to think she's going to pay for something I could have saved her from and didn't, I said. Easy now, Federico, something your brother could have saved her from and didn't, she pointed out, It's funny, You're still trying to take responsibilities off Lourenço's back, you keep thinking these mistakes are never his, That he's the unimpeachable one, the man with no defects, she chastised me. I told her that wasn't true. Fine, This isn't the moment for blaming anyone, Bárbara said. I put the question again of what I should do about Roberta. I'm not really sure, Federico, I've seen Roberta maybe three times since she stopped being a kid, You said you saw fear in her eyes, Being afraid in the situation she's in is normal, That's not what you need to worry about, It's the anger that's likely to be growing inside that fear, Anger, that good old friend of yours and of your father's, But I have to say, you did the right thing coming down when your brother called, It's important you being near Roberta, Important you being near him, Lourenço's busy with all the activity at the club, And with this business of his being trainer for the state basketball team until the end of the year, like you said, That's a lot for him, There's no way he'll be able to support her as much as she's going to need, It's time to show her some affection, And you are, without a shadow of a doubt, more than able to show her sufficient affection for both Lourenço and yourself, Bárbara said. I'm feeling powerless, insecure, to tell

119

the truth, And I feel totally pointless when I'm like this, you know, I said. Look, she said, and she sighed, her expression showing me just how hard she was struggling to deal with this unexpected situation as best she could, It's a critical, painful process, Federico, And it's going to affect you, There's no way it could be any different, But, believe me, it's important for you to go through it, To be absorbed by it, Your niece's situation could end up acting as a mirror, in which you might be able to see yourself more clearly, and that's stressful, sure, but it could also be beneficial, It's a process that might help you to understand why you've never managed to centre yourself emotionally, and, who knows, it might close a cycle, A cycle inside that heart in there, Let's be optimistic, and she touched my chest. I put my hand on her hand, but she was already drawing back. I'm going to hope that this moment, which is so very critical, might bring you the silence you've always needed, the silence I've always said you needed to find, some way to help cancel out a lot of the noise you've got surrounding you, that's surrounding you and which you cling to, she said. Your old theory, I replied. No, It's more than that, Fedê, It's a fact, You collect noise, every new noise you encounter you drag it over and add it to the rest, so certain that accumulating all that noise will somehow be fuel for your escape, but it doesn't work, And I've told you this before, In excess the only thing you'll find will be a mirage, a promise that will never be fulfilled. Her statements about my not being able to centre myself emotionally, and about my not being able to find the necessary silence in my life, struck my heart like a hammer on an anvil. Perhaps at some point, tomorrow or in the coming days, you'll be able to show Roberta that nobody has control of the flow of their life, nobody has the power to choose what will or won't knock us down, that there are these inexplicable moments that will always come along to overwhelm us, come to mess everything up, do away with everything, even our way of life, And that this, when it happens, will need to be processed, absorbed, and she fell silent. But, objectively speaking, I asked, what should I do tomorrow. I think the best thing you'll be able to do tomorrow, objectively speaking, starts today, And it's trying to relax, trying to give that head of yours a rest, As for me, I'd suggest I give you all some help remotely, by phone, We can try to monitor her condition, And I can give a few tips based on what you tell me, Tomorrow I only see people in practice at the end of the day, I'm seeing clients from six to nine in the evening, so up till about four thirty I'll be free, Bárbara said. And we heard knocks on the glass of the party room door. It was her boyfriend standing on the other side with two glasses of red wine. Bárbara got up, opened the door. Hi, Federico, said the boyfriend, I've brought some wine down for the two of you, my love, and to say you're not to worry, Professor Megale and I are taking care of serving the folks upstairs, he said. Bárbara took the glasses and kissed his cheek, Thank you, Rafael, she said. Thank you, Rafael, I said. He nodded. Another ten minutes and I'll come up and join you, she said. If you want to come up later and join us, Federico, you'd be welcome, he said. Thank you, Rafael, I said. Another ten minutes, Bárbara repeated. And he walked out, leaving the door open. Nice kid, I said. I thought the age difference would be a problem, but you know it really isn't, He's a great companion, He's a radiant person, He comforts me, calms me, and she handed me one of the glasses. I thanked her. Don't let the anger take control of your niece, Bárbara resumed, Try, just do whatever you feel is within your grasp, she said, Anger never turns into solace, she stressed. I know, I said. A father's crusade can drown his son, always remember that, she said. It's complicated when it happens to someone close to us, I said, If she gets taken to prison her life's going to, Just imagine, That hellish place, I said sadly. Look, There's no way of knowing what's going to happen, Federico, And please don't start with all the projecting, with the second-guessing, And I know it's obvious, but I have a duty to remind you of that, she said. Lourenço told me she's talking about dropping Maths to take Journalism, he says she wants to be a reporter, I said. I think choosing the Journalism course could be a good sign, she said, and she got to her feet, Let's go up, You'll like the crowd up there, Eat something with us, Finish that wine, Then go get some rest, Those bags under your eyes are really deep, Come on, please, she said. Forget it, I've been too much bother already, But can I just stay here a few minutes on my own and finish this glass, Would that be OK, I asked. But then I'll feel guilty for leaving you by yourself, she said. You know me, You know you have nothing to feel guilty about, You know I'll be fine, It's just I want to process what we've talked about, Really I didn't come here to bother you for no reason, It's just that I'm worried, Trying not to lose my balance, I said. You know I'm always here if you need me, she said, she waved by opening and closing her fingers and then returned to the company of her guests, taking her glass along without having had so much as a single sip.

I drank a bit of the wine, good wine, took out my phone, made a list in my head: first Andiara, then Micheliny, and finally Eduardo, Dr Eduardo Travolta.

I texted Hi to Andiara.

I texted Micheliny Hi, Micheliny. Can you talk?

I'm in Porto Alegre, can you talk? I texted Travolta.

Hi Federico. U OK? Micheliny wrote.
    How'd it go at the commission today? I wrote.
    We missed you.
    It's not that bad.
    Ruy and I are more and more isolated on the question of the software . . . Ricardo didn't show again, I think he's given up.
    I sent you the message bc I don't think I'll be able to go back to Brasília next wk for our meeting on Tues.
    Are things serious there?
    Family problems. I don't know if I'll be back in time for the Thurs meeting. We'll see how things pan out here.
    Not good for you to miss so much. Your contribution is important.
    I'm the one who talks least.
    But you're the one most suspicious of the commission. It's good having somebody sceptical here.
    I don't trust this government, Micheliny.
    Sure.
    Sorry, I don't want to put you in a tight spot.

Us on the commission are doing something important, Federico.

I admire your position. I'm here if you need anything.

Same to you, she wrote.

We'll talk, I wrote.

She sent some emojis.

In the movies just ending will call when I'm out, Travolta wrote.

OK, I wrote.

Travolta sent an emoji.

I finished the wine in three swigs. I got up, turned off the party room light, went out, walked over to the doorman, asked him to pass the glass on to Bárbara, thanked him, wished him a good shift. He thanked me, unlocked the door. I left the building, walked down Álvaro Alvim to Dona Leonor and then to the corner with Protásio Alves, where Al Nur was, the restaurant where Bárbara and I used to go regularly at the end of the nineteen nineties. I went in, asked for three meat sfihas and a bottle of guaraná. Travolta sent me a message on WhatsApp saying he was out and asking if he could call me. I said not to bother, that I'd call him, and I did. He was with his fiancée. It was funny hearing his voice saying fiancée. I asked if he knew some place in Partenon frequented by students, where the clientele was young people between eighteen and twenty-five. You want to bone a university student, Fucking hell, That's some real mega-Indian-style shit, you dirty bastard, Bastard, he said. I told him not to talk crap, it was nothing like that, I just wanted to know what the new Partenon was like, to know where the university students from my neighbourhood were hanging out, there weren't any places like that in our day. He laughed, said it was just as well things had changed. I thought about saying Yeah, things really have changed, and the proof of how much they'd changed was precisely him, the laziest slacker in my brother's gang having become a respected traumatologist, but no, I let it go. There's this place opened a couple of years ago, the Guitar Man, which is a bar with a stage, where they have loads of cool gigs, It's a samba-rock bar, but mostly what you get there is rap, Suzana and I have been there a few times, It's on Santa Maria, he said. I told him I'd pop over there. He said I should be smart, go in a cab, he made a point of reminding me that, unlike me, he was still in the neighbourhood and, for that reason, as a resident of the neighbourhood, what he had to tell me was that I should be careful, most of all in the area where the club was, in São José, an area bordering Partenon, considered by everyone in the eastern zone to be a part of Greater Partenon. He explained that São José was no joke, that just the same as the rest of Porto Alegre, a city in which a thug could stroll into the airport and execute anyone he dislikes in cold blood in the departure lounge, walk out again and disappear without the slightest trouble, you shouldn't be taking chances there after 10 p.m. I thanked him for his advice, said I hoped to meet up with him soon. He gave me his traditional take it easy and I replied with a take it easy yourself. We hung up. I ate the sfihas, I didn't finish drinking all the guaraná in the bottle. I asked for the bill, paid, left. On Protásio Alves I took the first taxi that came past. The driver was dressed full gaúcho, a real southerner properly looking the part, with the boots, bombacha trousers, guaiaca belt, white shirt, red neckerchief, felt hat with a leather chinstrap. I asked if he was like one of those old Maragato revolutionaries, or just a supporter of Internacional, the football team. He replied he was neither one nor the other, he said he liked red because red was a good colour to wear when you worked nights like he did, it was the colour of Saint George's cloak, a colour that warded off harm, and he asked if I'd been to that year's Farroupilha Camp in Parque Harmonia yet. The fair was set up on the seventh of September and ran to the twentieth, which was Gaúcho Day, a day of pride in being a southerner, a day commemorating the Revolução Farroupilha, the so-called Ragamuffin Revolution. I said I'd never been. He said I was missing out because the energy there was really healthy, the gaúcho brotherhood celebrating the efforts made in one of the most epic and bloodiest wars in our country's history. Bloody, Only if you mean for the blacks, who were betrayed by the rural landowners and the political leaders, I said. I don't believe in that version, he said, I've got dark skin and I feel very well represented in the Farroupilha Week celebrations, The slaves fought alongside the whites and they fought for freedom and gave their lives for a Rio Grande do Sul free from oppression, a state free from the exploitation of the Empire, We didn't bow down, That's what matters, he argued. I do respect your version, And I think commemorating the twentieth of September is a lovely thing, but the truth is we lost the war and if there was anything bloody about it, it was only really bloody for the poor, the enslaved, who were, yeah, it's true, betrayed by Canabarro and by the other leaders of the revolution like Bento Gonçalves, I said, and I noticed we were on Bento Gonçalves Avenue at just that very moment. Bento Gonçalves died a rich man, he even left slaves to his heirs, as recent historians have shown, And the war, it wasn't one of the bloodiest wars, There were a lot of other and bloodier conflicts in Brazil, Another thing that's not true is the version of it being a revolution initiated to defend great ideals, I mean maybe that story could make sense if you wanted to use it as some sort of fable, but today we know there were a lot of bad things that happened on the Farroupilha side too, I said. The taxi drove past the Catholic university and a little further up turned into Santa Maria. And just one last thing, senhor, I said, seeing he wasn't liking what I was saying one bit, We also know today that the amnesty decree and all the other decrees from the Empire that benefited the rebel leaders, the southern élite, they weren't in any way gestures towards the freedom of the slaves who were fighting, They were put at the Empire's disposal, treated like the enslaved men they were, like a commodity, I said. The taxi driver stopped outside the bar, told me the fare, I paid, thanked him. I bade him goodnight. And he didn't answer.

When I went into the Guitar Man they were playing a very little-known number from the Jam Pony Express DJs over the PA. Reading the posters stuck up in the entrance hall I learned that the band who were going to play that night were Partenon 80, the trip to the Guitar Man wasn't just going to be a bit of snooping into what Roberta might have been doing on a Thursday night, she who when talking to me at my parents' house three years earlier, precocious as she was, had said she wasn't all that keen on areas like Cidade Baixa and Bom Fim, when I asked if she went to Bom Fim a lot, said she was more into the bars in the Historic Centre and in Partenon. Funkadelic played after Jam Pony Express, and after Funkadelic came Public Enemy. On the walls there were loads of photos, loads of album covers, magazine features, gig posters for various black bands, for various black musicians. I got a guaraná at the bar and hung around there just watching the coming and going. It really was a student bar. By the patrons' attire and behaviour, and because three or four of them were wearing hoodies with the PUC logo, I assumed it was a bar much more commonly frequented by PUC students than kids from other institutions like UFRGS or Unisinos, but I had no way of knowing for sure. When I finished my soft drink and went to ask for another, I noticed there was this really skinny guy, about my height, at the opposite end of the bar, staring at me conspicuously. I asked for the guaraná, handed over my tab and stared back. He didn't get intimidated, but came right over. I tried to prepare myself for whatever might happen. Hi, he said. I didn't reply. Aren't you the brother of Lourenço, the basketball guy, the União basketball coach, he asked. Why, I said. Take it easy, I don't want any trouble, My name's Caio, I'm one of the owners of the bar, he said. Yeah, I'm his brother, yes, I replied. You're Federico, right, he said. I relaxed slightly. The server handed me the guaraná and the tab. Your brother's a real solid guy, he taught basketball to my current girlfriend's two kids when he was doing Phys Ed at Santo Antônio, they love Lourenço to this day, he said. Lourenço hasn't taught at that school for a while now, I said. I know, he's only at União now, he said. Right, I said. I know him from over at the Little Goat, You know what I'm saying, right, I'm one of those scrawny little brats who used to wander round there in the earliest hours of the morning to get a toastie, a piglet, that's what we called the little snack pack Billy used to make us, Billy, That guy was a pal, all heart, He used to give me food without ever making a fuss, and I tried to help out however I could, it was like three years I stayed round there, then I set up something else, But Billy was the guy who stopped me becoming a street kid, He was always giving me advice, Your brother used to give me advice too, he said. And I realised that, from the way he was talking and looking at me, the guy was stoned, high, wild, whatever. Lourenço was the man, You know what I'm saying, right, and I'd been using a bit of shoemaker's glue, but I remember you all, Everyone who used to come and get snacks at the Little Goat, From all the different crowds, he said pensively, You see I'm good at retaining names and features, But with Lourenço, even if I wasn't good at that, I'd have known his name and face forever, Generous guy, He'd show up at the Little Goat in some really fucking nice threads, some nice sportswear, some imported sneakers. I remember no one had imported sneakers in those days, let alone in Partenon, It was total class seeing your brother, There's a good reason he worked as a model, He was just cool, He didn't avoid me, He wasn't afraid of swapping a few ideas with me, He didn't treat me like I was a leper, he said, touched despite his agitation, You went there sometimes too, didn't you, he asked. I went a few times, I replied. Right, 'cause I got you too, but you were more unsociable, he said. I didn't interact as much, that's all, I replied. Right, But let me tell you, Managing to get out of the house, going down Humberto de Campos, to go to Billy's Xis Van, Feeling cool, Those were the high points of my week, he said. I nodded so he could see I understood. You know what saved me, What saved me, truly, was my poor troubled mother died, That's the truth, My blessed and crazy in the head old ma, may God keep her, died, and me and my sister went to live with our aunt, here in Vila João Pessoa, Our aunt, who was bringing up three little 'uns already, who wasn't on good terms with my mother but who took us in, our aunt who put us on track, She worked for a PDT party councillor and later became kind of his partner, she managed to get us into school, to get us healthcare, My aunt became the most engaged sort of militant, my three cousins and my sister and me too, So I started to get involved with the demands being made by the communities in the area here, from Santo Antônio to Lomba do Pinheiro, Aparício Borges, Jardim Carvalho, Agronomia, Tuca, Morro da Cruz, Later I switched party from the PDT to the PT and I started getting more involved with cultural stuff, with some bands, some theatre groups, events like Porto Alegre On Stage, and I enrolled in the administration faculty, Later I dropped out of the course in my third year to open up an event production company, And life went on, And I ended up here, a partner in a music venue in São José, he said. That's a nice trajectory, I replied. I'm a fan of your brother's, Lourenço never moved away, Lourenço's not all theory, Lourenço just is, he said. Yeah, I said. Is he still living in Jardim Botânico, he asked. Yeah, I replied. He may have left the area, but he never stopped coming back to the hood to see his friends again, the guy said. What time does the show start, I asked. He checked the time. In half an hour at most, he replied. Can I ask you a question, he said. Yes, I said. You, OK, who's all educated, and who's a doctor, who writes articles for the papers, magazines, who's presented as some kind of leader in some videos for the Black Cause on YouTube, this big megastar, living in Brasília, who's on some big-shot commission set up by this bullshit new government up there, that's fine, I'm not going to judge you for that, You, Federico, What are you doing in a bar in São José, he asked. I came to, I tried to answer. He didn't let me. I read some recent interviews of yours, he said, You're real articulate. And then my phone vibrated. I checked it. It was a WhatsApp message from Andiara. It vibrated again and again. Look, man, this talk of ours is great, I said, but I've got to look at some messages that have just come in, and I stepped away.

Only just seen your message. Missing you, Andiara wrote, followed by an emoji.

I'm in a bar you wdnt believe, I wrote.

All OK there?

All OK, just wanted to talk to you a bit.

Not in any state right now. Went to the meeting of the commission. Feeling more and more like I'm in a tower of Babel. I'm the only person still arguing for self-ID.

If that's your opinion, stick with it.

In the afternoon went to the library in the Congress building & stayed till it closed. Went swimming after. Exhausted now. Kind of hung-over.

I'll call you, let's talk a bit.

No way, I'm taking half a Rivotril and switching off. I'm up early tomorrow, I've got to slow down, body's wrecked but head's going ten to the dozen.

I just wanted to hear your voice.

If we start talking we'll talk for an hour at least & it'll be past my bedtime. I need to go to bed. Emoji. Call me tomorrow.

OK. Get some rest. Kisses.

Missing you, she wrote.

You too, I wrote.

She sent another emoji.

When I returned to the bar and to my guaraná, Caio was waiting for me with a bottle of vodka and two shot glasses. Man, I pre-empted him, That's cool, but I'm not going to drink, I'm just going to watch the band do their set and that's it, I said. He poured the vodka into the glasses anyway. Come on, you're in my bar, You really going to insult me like that, are you, he insisted. I took the glass. We clinked, we drank. Another round, he said, and filled his glass. Thanks, and I took my glass off the counter before he'd had the chance to serve me. Just one more, So I can say that Federico, Lourenço's brother, came to my bar and we had not one, but two, Come on, And then we'll take a selfie for me to post on the Guitar Man Insta. Man, thanks, but it's all good, I'm watching the Partenon 80 show then I'm going, I said. He looked at me with glazed eyes. Bro, let me tell you this, You kind of think you're something special, right, Must be fun to pose as spokesman for the crowd, king of abstract theory, the leading man, Tarzan Lord of the Apes, Go on, tell me, I've come to check on all the chimps, Have a bit of a laugh with the chimps, he looked around and then back at me, While you were on your phone I got to remembering, And I thought it weird you being Lourenço's brother, because he's black and man you're seriously fucking white, And I thought if you were brothers, despite him being dark-brown coloured and you white like a heart of palm, if he's cool then you must be cool too, And that's why that one time I tried to start a conversation with you, but you looked at me oh so superior, like someone who thought he was better than me, who thought he was better than everybody, and you just said one line to me, Do you remember, he asked, No, I'm sure you don't, You said you didn't give to beggars, Man, you said to a ten-year-old kid, who just wanted to ask how your brother was doing, that you didn't give to beggars, Do you have any idea how arrogant you are, You were what, maybe sixteen years old, Seventeen, you had your health, you had a father and mother, a father and mother who must have given you everything, you had brains, And you couldn't chat with a kid who just wanted a bit of attention, he said. Caio, look, I'm not here to hurt anyone, If I messed up with you three decades back, I'm sorry, I think I got a bit better between then and now, And I'm sorry, Really, I said, But I've come here, to your bar, because I heard it was a cool place, Because in my day there wasn't a cool place like this round here, here in the neighbourhood, I said. Here in the neighbourhood, he said, Right, the neighbourhood, man, Tell me what work you've done for the black kids here in Partenon these last ten years, these last fifteen years, he asked, Man, you don't do crap for your neighbourhood, he said, I got out of the shit because I got given a chance and I didn't let go, he said. That's great, I replied. And having got out of the shit is what gives me permission to tell any sucker I see, when I meet one who he thinks he's really killing it, that he's just not, he said. Thank you for the tip, I said. Man, you're so stuck-up, Federico, always were, Look at the colour of your skin, look at your hair, the way you wear that slicked-back hair you got, You got that white shell of yours, that totally fucking access-all-areas skin, You're never going to understand what it is to be black, to be a poor fucker getting hassled twenty-four seven on your street, in your neighbourhood, in your city, You don't know, Totally stuck-up, And so, buddy, you'd best not relax, Today you're here, you're all good here in the Guitar Man, you're going to see the Eighty show, But don't you relax, and best lose that attitude of yours, that profound mental trip of yours as this righteous do-gooder, You're worthless, man, you don't know what it is to be part of the race, Don't start getting ideas about being some defender of the cause, you cretin palm-heart opportunist piece of shit, And think three times before you come back here again, 'cause if you do, and I'm here, the shit could end up real bad for you, Keep your wits about you, and he threw back the shot glass of vodka he'd already poured. I gave him a pat on the shoulder and an OK great I'll see you around and moved away from the bar, headed for the back of the room. The show started fifteen minutes later. I watched it. There in the Guitar Man. With lots of young people, lots of guys and girls who could have been Roberta. And that Caio guy stayed in the same place at the bar, drinking his vodka and clapping enthusiastically at the end of each number until the show ended.

The telephone in the hallway, one of the four telephones dotted around the house, the one on a wall fitting, like a kind of boarding-house phone, the loudest one in the house, rings many times. My mother must have gone out, I think she mentioned she needed to go to the seamstress on Antônio Ribeiro to drop off the bag of our clothes that need mending. I get out of bed, open my bedroom door and, in the hallway, I answer the phone. It's Joel Fearless Fly. I tell him Lourenço isn't home. He says it's me he wants to talk to, he says it was Lourenço who gave him the tip to call me, he tells me he's found himself stuck with three tickets for a party that's going to happen at the Leopoldina tonight, he explains that he bought four because he was going to go with his cousins who were meant to be coming from Nova Prata, but their mother got sick, sounds like she's having serious trouble with her heart, which should have got better by now but didn't, and anyway the three of them decided not to travel, so he asks if I wouldn't like to buy a ticket off him, to help him out a bit, so he isn't left out of pocket, he says the party's going to be good, he gives me a load of details. I ask the price. He answers. I say I want two, but I want them at a discount. He stays quiet for a second and then he says he can give me a discount of ten per cent. I say I'll take the tickets. He says it's a deal and talks about a load of other things that have nothing to do with the party but which are funny, Fearless Fly has a salesman's gift of the gab like a proper actual used-car salesman, the kind who worries about giving his customer total satisfaction even when the sale is already concluded, even when he hasn't negotiated as well as he'd hoped to negotiate, then he says he's got to come round to the neighbourhood anyway and that he'll drop the tickets off at the house. I say there's no need, that I was thinking of going out around three in the afternoon and only coming back around seven. But like any business-man who knows he's doing business with a reliable payer, he uses the technique of needing to hand the merchandise over to the buyer once and for all in order to leave it quite clear that the deal is done and there's no way back, he says there's no problem at all him stopping by the house before three. I say I'll wait for him then, but that I think I'll only be able to get hold of the money later, that I'll pay him tonight. He says he's on his motorbike and that sometime before three o'clock he'll leave the tickets in the mailbox of my house so he doesn't waste any time, so I don't have to come out to meet him, and he thanks me for my support. We hang up. I stay in the hallway a few minutes, just standing there, looking at the telephone. Then I go to my mother's studio room, her own private little space, the place she slips away to in order to hide from us, to take her daily reward-vacation from us, I pick up a piece of three-hundred-gram Canson paper, one of the ones she divides with a ruler into eight parts and leaves piled up on one corner of her table, expensive paper, made from cotton fibres, textured only on the obverse, made to last for centuries, I return to my room, sit down at my desk, pick up one of the uni-ball pens that she, my mother, gave me as a present when I passed my college entrance exam, I get out the record of Bowie's *Let's Dance*, the best album I bought last year, I take the liner notes out of the sleeve, I read the lyrics of the song 'Let's Dance', I get the Canson card, I write and cross out and write:

~~If you say run, I'll run with you~~
Se tu disser escape, eu escapo junto contigo

Then I get out a standard mailing envelope with the typical interleaved green and yellow printed on the edges, the same envelope into which I'm going to stick one of the invitations for tonight's party at the Leopoldina, and I put the card inside, feeling slightly more inclined to take a shower and, at around three, to go out.

My cell phone rang at six forty-seven in the morning. Are you in Brasília, asked my father on the other end of the line. Morning, Dad, I said, already trying to be disarming. Good morning, Federico, he said, and I could hear I'd succeeded in disarming him. I'm in Porto Alegre, I replied. When did you get in, he asked. Yesterday afternoon, I replied after a moment's hesitation, sensing he was going to ask why I hadn't called to say I was in town. But he didn't. Are you with your brother, is what he asked. No, but I'm meeting up with him soon, Right now I'm at an ibis here in Garibaldi, close to Farrapos, He said he was coming in the car to get me at eight, I said. So you're in Porto Alegre, he said. I'm in Porto Alegre, Dad, I confirmed. I've just read a story in the newspaper about Roberta, he said. Yeah, Dad, that's right, me and Lô thought it best not to tell you or Mum anything, we thought it would all get sorted out yesterday, But unfortunately it didn't, I said. I know, I called the police jail a little while ago, And I identified myself, And asked how she was doing, he said. What did they tell you, I asked. The guy who answered, and it's just as well he knew who I was, told me she's doing fine, he said. Yeah, they're treating her well, They haven't sent her to prison yet, which, as you know, that's a good thing, I said. You're helping your brother, he didn't need to ask, but he asked. Yeah, That's why I came from Brasília, I said. You did the right thing, he said. I'll stop by there later to see you and Mum, I said. Check that the lawyer is doing his work right, my father insisted. He's good, You can rest easy, Dad, he's good, I assured him. If you need to use my name, you can, If you need to call me, you can, he said. Have you already spoken to Lourenço, I asked. I wanted to talk to you first. To find out, I said. Yes, to find out, he said. I'm here, Dad, I said, wanting to calm him down. I'm going to call your brother, Wonder if he's awake already, my father said. I'm sure he's up already, But I don't know if it wouldn't be better to wait and call in the afternoon when we have a clearer idea of what's going to happen to Beta, I said. That might be better, don't you think, he asked. I think so, I replied. So I'll call him after lunch, he said. And Mum, is she already up, I asked. No, Célia's still sleeping, he said. When she wakes up and you tell her what happened, if she then wants to know about Roberta, tell her to call me, All right, I said. All right, he said. We're going to sort this all out, Dad, And we're going to do it today, I said. All right, son, he said. Lots of love, Dad, And give Mum a kiss too, I said. Call me, he said. In his voice, more pronounced than the other times when we'd talked on the phone, I heard the sharp, almost metallic timbre that had appeared in recent years, and he hung up.

Outside the Police Headquarters jail, standing in one of the spaces beside the five vehicles parked on the sidewalk, Augusto notified us that the duty captain had turned down our request to talk to Roberta for a few minutes. That the vagueness as to her fate was continuing, since the maximum seventy-two hours after her detention had not yet passed, was something I could almost accept, but not being able to meet her to talk for a moment was more than I could handle. Apparently less frustrated than me at our not having been able to meet her, my brother was in a different mood, what he could or couldn't accept didn't match with my own inclinations. He put his hands on the lawyer's shoulders and, without registering how ludicrous his insistence would sound, he asked how, for Christ's sake, how could a judge take such a long time to decide about granting a release. Without the confidence he'd had the day before and freeing himself from the weight of Lourenço's hands on his shoulders, Augusto said that criminal procedural law was tortuous, that it depended a lot on various often unpredictable factors, on the administrative logistics of each specific place, that Porto Alegre, to those observing it from the outside, gave the impression of being one of the most organised places in the country, one of the most civilised places, but it wasn't, He explained that, in practice, the bureaucratic process depended on each judge's understanding, each senior officer's, each prosecutor's, that there was a certain degree of predictability, but that afterwards, if what had been predicted didn't happen, then it just turned into a whole big Everybody-throw-everything-up-in-the-air-and-see-what-happens, and if you didn't like how things turned out, you could resort to higher authorities, but he said what mattered was not allowing the administrative procedure of an arrest in flagrante to turn into a labyrinth, a labyrinth with no way out, that the first and most basic task

of any good lawyer was to make sure his client always had
a way out.

Of the five vehicles that had been parked on the police
building sidewalk only one remained, a Fiat Palio. Propped
up against the bodywork of the Palio's hood, an officer from
the military police, a guy probably in his early twenties, was
busily fiddling with a cell phone while he smoked a cigarette.
Augusto was also fiddling with his phone when my brother
asked if it wouldn't be a good idea to go in and ask the police
if they had any news. Yes, good idea, Augusto said. And my
brother looked at him with an expression that said Well go
on then. His condition as tormented father paying dearly
for Augusto's advice gave my brother the right to, at certain
critical moments, exercise his prerogative of impatience.
I'll be back soon, the lawyer said, and he went inside. I told
Lourenço I was going to stretch my legs, he was to call me if
anything happened. I walked to the front of the Institute of
Forensic Medicine, which also housed the main forensics
lab of the Rio Grande do Sul civil police, which was the
building adjacent to the police jail. The façade was just as it
had been in the days when my father had worked there as the
state's director-general of forensics. The entrance had been
modernised, but it wasn't really all that different from the
entrance I'd known. A group of five people was coming out of
the building: a man in his seventies, three striking women in
their forties who looked very like one another, and a teenage
boy. The man was trying to comfort one of the women, the
teenager walked behind them all with tears in his eyes. And
it was impossible not to compare the situation of the people

141

visiting those two buildings on Ipiranga Avenue, either to see relatives who'd been arrested or to see relatives who were dead. My aim, which had been to walk to the corner with Santana and then to the corner with São Luís and only then come back was replaced with a new determination to stay where I was, overtaken by empathy for those five people, observing their actions, waiting to see what they would do next. The noise of the cars speeding down the four lanes of Ipiranga Avenue and my distance from them, fifteen metres by my calculation, prevented my getting a better idea of what they were talking about. One of the women, seemingly the oldest, took out her phone and made a call. While she talked, the others listened. And, trying not to be too intrusive, from a distance, I watched them. The woman started screaming into her phone, and I was able to get a rough idea of what was going on. A murder. The woman was still on the phone, the other four remained inert, watching her every gesture, listening to her every word. The minutes passed and I only disconnected from them finally when my own phone rang and I heard my brother's voice telling me to come back, because Augusto had some news.

Roberta was going to be taken, along with a group of detainees from the police station, to the Central Courthouse, where her detention hearing was to take place. The referral had been determined by the presiding judge, and the employees at the police station already knew, most likely, about the decision, but it was the duty captain, the third one we were dealing with, who'd decided to release the information, and only just this instant. Lourenço asked the lawyer whether he had any idea what time Roberta would be leaving the police

station and what time her hearing would be. He said detention hearings tended to be held one after another, twenty to
thirty per morning, that they had an order, a sequence, but
it was hard to specify what time Roberta's would be, that
there was no point just waiting there for her to be driven
off, that it would be best for us to head over to the Central
Courthouse and wait there. And before I could ask whether
my brother and I would be allowed to attend the hearing, he
added the piece of information that it'd taken him a while not
because of the news of the detention hearing, but because of
having run into an inspector friend of his, an old friend he'd
drifted apart from over the years but who, despite the lack
of more frequent contact, retained for him, Augusto, a high
regard, a regard that was mutual, an old inspector with good
access through the various levels of operational hierarchy,
who knew the structure, had all the information, the files of
everybody on the force, especially the ones occupying posi-
tions of power, and who wasn't going to refuse to say what
needed to be said if he, Augusto, asked for a frank answer to
the question of who it was in the upper ranks who was going
after Roberta. And that's just what happened. The inspector
revealed that the officer who'd taken an interest in Roberta
was the head of the civil police's Office of Intelligence and
Strategic Affairs, Deputy Director Pederiva Setúbal, a guy
with few friends, thorough, dedicated, known for arriving
in the late morning and, invariably, working till after eight
at night, including on weekends, and who, owing to the
important post he occupied, knew about everything that
happened in the civil as well as the military police, and sooner
or later was going to become chief of police, not through the

traditional route of operational politicking, but because he was focused and tough on himself as few officers tended to be. Lourenço asked for the officer's full name. Augusto said it was Douglas Pederiva Setúbal, and I took out my phone and typed Douglas Pederiva Setúbal into Google. There wasn't a lot of information about him, what little I found was mostly related to his activities at the Civil Police Academy. No picture of his face, no video. Then I went to Facebook and found an account that wasn't accessible to the public, and on it, in his profile photo, his face.

As we travelled over to the Central Courthouse in Lourenço's van, me in the passenger seat, the lawyer in the back, I was considering the merits of telling my brother that this officer in charge of the civil police's Intelligence and Strategic Affairs division was one of the guys we'd had a fight with outside the Leopoldina Juvenil in nineteen eighty-four, the one in the polo shirt with the Grêmio crest embroidered on the sleeves, the only one of them I've never forgotten. If he was as methodical and well informed as Augusto said, he surely knew whose daughter Roberta was, whose granddaughter she was, whose niece she was and, surely, he wasn't going to just let her go scot-free. Owing to the speciality and importance of the division he headed up, he presumably had the operational capability to call in the criminal investigation for himself and charge my niece any way he liked. Terrorist, terrorist's accomplice, whatever, the guy wasn't going to stop till he'd fucked her over, fucked her over so as to fuck me over and fuck my brother over. Lourenço stopped at the lights at Ipiranga and Praia de Belas. A teenage couple walked over the crossing, hand in hand, smiling, her wearing a Grêmio T-shirt, him an Internacional T-shirt.

Only Lourenço was allowed in to attend the hearing. It was the presiding judge's policy to authorise the presence of only one relative per detainee. The proceedings were expected to take no more than fifteen minutes, but ended up lasting a little over half an hour, because the prosecutor, according to the lawyer's subsequent report, wanted to get tough and even floated the theory that Roberta could have been in cahoots with the other students who took part in the protest and who were also arrested in the raid, students who had been carrying suspicious chemical products as well as pamphlets that were no less suspicious. The judge didn't accept this theory, he said sufficient facts had not been presented, at least not as yet, that there was no evidence to sustain any classification of her behaviour as terrorist activity, a theory that might have been suggested to the prosecuting attorney by this officer Douglas, Augusto speculated, and, before granting provisional release on bail, setting the value of the bail at ten thousand reais, he made it clear that the gun in question, the .32 calibre revolver with expired ammo, even though it was the property of the military police, hadn't been fit to fulfil its mechanical function, its destiny as a firearm, those were the words the lawyer used, and, therefore, had posed no real danger. Roberta wasn't released at once, it was only after the final hearing of the whole series of hearings scheduled for that morning and early afternoon that she, along with some of the other detainees, since many were going to the central prison, would be driven back to the police cells, where she would only be given her freedom after Lourenço had received the bail payment slip, gone to the closest Banrisul branch, withdrawn the ten thousand reais, returned to the police station and presented the proof of deposit for attaching to the proceedings.

It was four fifteen in the afternoon when we left the police station with Roberta. While Lourenço and his daughter talked on their own, I asked the lawyer what restrictions the girl would be subject to. He said there were no significant restrictions, that the judge, in his decision, hadn't ordered the withholding of her passport, hadn't forbidden her from going out at night, from leaving the city, there wasn't much to worry about, he said, the thing was for her to stay out of trouble in the meantime, she couldn't commit any crimes, stuff like that, or be away from her home for longer than eight days. I thanked him for his help. Seeing that Lourenço and Roberta were getting pretty emotional at their reunion, Augusto asked me to tell my brother that he'd be available to clarify any doubts that might arise, that he needed to run in order to help one of his assistants, who was advising on another case that initially hadn't seemed too complicated, but which was proving to be quite complicated indeed. The labyrinth, I said. He smiled. We shook hands. He waved to Lourenço and Roberta from a distance and headed towards the main road, where he managed to hail a passing cab.

After Lourenço had vigorously refused to explain to Roberta how a man who'd always been against the possession and the carrying of firearms had come to have one in the house,

Roberta got up from the dining table without another word, went to her room and locked herself inside. I told Lourenço he should maybe leave her alone for the time being, not to pressure her, it was being pressured that had made her confront him. He just looked towards the windowpane, contemplating the vestiges of the daylight. I started to gather up the dishes, the glasses, the pan with the rest of the chicken and rice I'd prepared. After I picked up the bottle top to the Fanta Orange that was on the tablecloth, Roberta was addicted to Fanta Orange, screwed it back on, put the bottle to one side and started to gather up the tablecloth, Lourenço raised a hand for me to stop. That's fine, Federico, Leave it, And you can forget about doing the washing-up, said Lourenço. If I cook, I wash up, I said. OK, bro, but you're in my house, Sit your ass there and settle down, he said. You think she's going to be OK, I asked. She is, yeah, she's just scared, Lourenço said. I'm going to make some tea, you want some tea, I asked. Just sit, Federico, Fuck, man, Just stop for a bit, he complained. I'm good, I said, and went over to the stove, got the kettle, filled it with water from the tap, put it on to heat up, Lô, I said quietly, there's something I need to say, It's just I don't like the way Roberta's behaving, Not about her having got up now the way she did and gone to her room, I mean generally, It's like she really believes that violence is the answer, Look, I'm sorry to be getting involved at this level, but I think it might be good for her to talk to somebody, You saw that at no point has she acknowledged she made a mistake, I said. Maybe she should talk to someone, he said. I'm going to call Bárbara, to ask her to come over, I suggested. Bárbara, Lourenço exclaimed, You never forget that woman, do you, old man. She's the best person I know to talk to Roberta, I said. Fine, but you don't seem to have realised it's Friday, buddy, Bárbara's probably got something on, You can't just call her out of nowhere and say come see my niece, he said. She's in practice until nine, If I ask her to stop by here, she'll come gladly, I said. You reckon, he asked. I talked to her yesterday, And I know she wouldn't say no to seeing Roberta, I said. Federico, Federico, You really can't get that woman out of your head, And I bet she can't forget you either, he said, Have you guys gotten over your differences, he asked. I talked briefly about my most recent encounters with Bárbara, about the parts of my history with her that he certainly didn't know, and then, because the conversation drifted to other things, about getting old without having somebody you really care about close by, somebody you can count on, we talked like two people who'd realised they had a debt to one another, who needed to become closer again, we talked until we realised that the kettle, which I'd left on a low flame, had been boiling for some time. I asked where he kept the teas. He got up, told me to forget about the tea, said he'd make a chimarrão for us. I roared with laughter like I hadn't laughed since arriving in Porto Alegre. Chimarrão at this time, After dinner, I asked. This isn't a normal day, he replied. I wasn't a big fan of drinking chimarrão, but I didn't refuse when the invitation was coming from Lourenço, because I knew he didn't like drinking it alone. These are some good leaves, he said, Nice and thick, From up in Palmeira das Missões, he said. Let's do it, I said, seeing that he had become enthusiastic. I pulled up a chair and sat down.

The pack of she-bears was formed in order to enable pro-
tracted pregnancies, my mother reads, and she hands me the
first of the sheets on which she's done sketches for the illustrations. In the bears' artificial uteruses the development of
the selected foetuses is perfected, she hands over the sheet
with the second sketch, Until the extended pregnancy is over,
the foetus being hosted is called pre-reinvigorated, Then it's
called reinvigorated, she hands me the third and fourth
sketches, Then at some point the idea of hope was added into
the Bears programme, and, interrupting the reading of her
notes, she looks at me with clear dissatisfaction. What is it,
Mum, I ask. The writer uses the word hope, But I prefer the
word soul, What do you think, she asks. Hope is good, but
I'd infinitely prefer soul, I reply. Then soul stays, she says,
and makes a note in the exercise book with the purple cover
that she tends to use to prepare the illustrations she's been
doing for the last three years for the books from Rocha
Rodrigues Publishers, where a former classmate from her
Júlio de Castilhos High School days works, a friend who,
knowing of her natural talent for drawing and painting,
though also aware of her position as a federal public employee,
invited her to collaborate. She's so careful, maybe even too

careful, because this is the first foreign book she's ever illustrated. You can keep going, I suggest. She hands me the fifth sketch. The bears carry the pre-reinvigorated foetus until the fourteenth month after conception, she hands over the sixth, One of the bears started to show flaws after the final general reprogramming of the bears, she reads, and passes me the seventh sketch. When is it that the foetuses get removed from the uterus of their natural mothers and implanted into the bears, I interrupt her. Implanted, she asks. I nod. At the end of the eighth month, she replies. I think that's a detail that should be on your list. She purses her lips with a grimace that means I think you're right, and she says, You're right. Do these bears know they're machines, I ask. Now she's looking at me as though to say You're interrupting me too often and she asks me to save my questions for later. The bear ran away from the Pre-reinvigorated Unit, she passes the eighth sketch, The bear killed anyone who tried to stop her running away, she passes the ninth, The bear, The bear, and she puts the sheaf of papers with the sketches to one side. What is it, Mum, I ask. It's not working, she admits. Is it difficult, I ask. This time it's really difficult, she says. Is it a difficult book, I ask. No, it's just a book that really affects me, It's a story that makes me want to stop everything and make a different story or to tell the story only with my illustrations, To a new script, A story of my own, I've been thinking about this since yesterday, And I think it's because of the subject matter, Any story that has motherhood in it affects me, she explains. Shouldn't sci-fi stories be light, I ask. No good story is ever light, Federico, No good story leaves out what's dense, what's heavy, she observes. Why don't you go straight into the pictures, Do it without a script this time. If the publishers challenge you, say you've produced a dialectic interpretation of the story, I suggest. She laughs. Go on, go ahead, get rid of the script this time, And I'm sure it'll flow more easily, I say, What could go wrong, I ask. I can't do it, son, You see I need to get my bearings very well before I start drawing, before I start painting, And I can't get a feel for it if, before I've started the work, the explanations aren't all complete in my head, each in its proper place, she says. Each one tidily in its own little drawer, I tease. Each explanation in its little drawer, right, she says. It must have been hard for you to put me and Lourenço in the same drawer, I say. We're a family, Federico, We're all four of us in the same drawer, she says. But if you hadn't had one dark son and one colourless son and, instead, you'd had two colourless sons or two dark sons, you never would have gone on banging that drum about us being a black family, I say, slightly aggressive. Do please try to be a bit more precise, child, she says. It's just the whole business about being black, Mum, It's that, sometimes, people think it's strange this thing about me asserting myself as black, me marking myself out as black, I explain. But you are black, a brown-skinned black, she points out, What's the big drama, she asks. What I'm trying to say is even if I tell people I'm black, it's not enough, Because I understand almost nothing about what it is to be black, in terms of culture, If it weren't for the Sunday barbecues we have, from time to time, with Dad's cousins, I wouldn't even properly know what real samba is, And I look at the way you guys brought me up, at the upbringing you and Dad gave me and Lourenço, and I see almost no blackness, nothing from the black world, almost nothing to do with black culture, and I realise I might be overdramatising a bit, but, my mother being my interlocutor, I can't help it. We are a black family, because you've always said we were black, Fine, But where is our blackness, We look more like a white family, we only have dealings with white people, all your colleagues and friends, everyone apart from the Moreiras and the Dos Arantes, are white people, Dad's colleagues and friends are white, We've shielded ourselves because I think that, deep down, that was the way for Dad to assert himself, To shield himself and not see anything to do with this business of race, ignoring the whites, ignoring the whites who don't like dark-skinned people, sure, But ignoring all the rest too, The blacks, Black culture, Racism, I say. What is it you're talking about, Federico, she asks. I'm talking about that word, even for us it's taboo, Racism, I'm talking about racism, Mum, I say. Look, I don't know where this is going, But if you're trying to give me a hard time for not letting our house get transformed into a headquarters of the black movement and not being full of flags and posters with Zumbi dos Palmares's face on them, with Free Nelson Mandela banners, well you can forget it right now, The answer is that I worry about our family, About the health of my children, Of my husband, I worry about our having peaceful lives and so I don't concern myself with militancy, I want a house where there's peace, because it's peace your father and your brother need, From the front door in, On our little patch of land, inside our house, is our place, Our ground, Our sacred space, Our space for being happy, for strengthening ourselves for life, and she sighs, Your father's in the police, You know all the risks he takes, You know the price he pays for not having to lower his eyes in front of his superiors, who are all white, yes, You know the price he pays for being honest, decent, too much sometimes, Your father doesn't think about colour, he doesn't look at colour, at the colour of his skin, at the colour of other people's skin, He doesn't waste time on that, Racism, He sees himself as a man, As a man who doesn't owe anyone anything, And he acts, He does, He lives, We do see the racism, We know what racism is, but we don't give in, Look, don't give yourself such a hard time, and she brings her hand to my head, smooths down my hair. I say nothing. Why are you being so insecure like this, she asks, Did someone say something to you, she asks, Did Bárbara, she asks. There is no more Bárbara, I say. Keep telling me what I want to hear, she says, and laughs. I'm serious, I say. Did something happen when you showed up for the selection at the barracks this morning, she asks. Of course not, I reply and pick up the sketches she hasn't shown me yet. Just get those daft ideas out of your head, son, Don't get all insecure, Insecurity doesn't suit you, It doesn't suit any of the three of you, she says. I cast my eyes over her drawings one by one. And it's just I know how people look up to us and how much they envy us, how many of them envy us, I say, But I think we could do more, OK, I'm black, but I don't know how to fight racism, I know how to get through it, I know how to assert myself, And I know my brother gets through it, But getting through it isn't the issue, The issue is putting an end to it, Mum, putting an end to this whole thing that's so wrong, this whole business that's a prison, I insist. Son, you're only seventeen, And I know at your age we all think we're going to fix the world, but it's not like that, she warns me. I don't want to feel black just because

153

I've learned to say I'm black, like a parrot, I want to really understand, I say. She gets up from her chair. Son, don't feel bad about it, don't waste your time feeling bad, she says. I hand her the sheets of paper and get up. I'm going to my room, I say. And don't let Bárbara make you suffer, she says, taking a firm hold of my chin. You can stay cool, Mum, I've given Bárbara a lot of things, but I haven't given her that power yet, I say. Listen, Before you go, Tell me if you know what time your brother went out this morning, she asks, Because today he wasn't supposed to have class for the first two periods, she says. I don't know, Mum, With the thing of my having to show up at the barracks today, he and I completely missed each other, I wasn't even home at the time he's usually up on Fridays, I say. He really needs to finish this crammer course, my mother says, And we've got to give him all the strength we can. I know, I've always got an eye on the young 'un, I say. And he has his eye on you, she replies as any attentive mother would. I leave her studio without saying any more, without looking back, and, as has happened before when I've invaded her space, I hear the sound of the bolt slotting into the door frame when she shuts the door behind me to get back to her own things, to isolate herself from us, to take her mini-vacation from us.

In the taxi that was supposed to take me from my brother's house, in Jardim Botânico, to the hotel, the driver, a man who looked to be about seventy, started talking about the new government as soon as we passed the corner of Ipiranga and Barão do Amazonas, talking about how much he believed in and was betting on the new government's ability to salvage the country's economy. He talked and every thirty seconds he activated the jet of the windscreen wipers, which, if it didn't hinder his visibility as driver certainly hindered my peace of mind as his passenger. As for his praise of the new government, I let him go on praising it, I thought my silence would discourage him, but it didn't, quite the opposite. Shortly before we arrived at the Planetarium corner, where we were to leave Ipiranga and take Ramiro towards Farrapos, he said that only the return of the military regime of exception from nineteen seventy-four, military regime of exception was the phrase he used, would really put an end to the widespread indolence that was preventing Brazil from prospering morally and economically. Everything has its limits. We turned onto Ramiro. In front of the UFRGS Biochem faculty building, I told him to pull over. He asked if I wasn't going to the hotel any more. I answered no and, without going into detail, thanked him, paid the fare, got out of the car. I could have walked to the taxi rank at the Hospital de Clinicas and got into the first cab that was free, but I didn't. I returned to Ipiranga, walked as far as the police building, checked the time. Seven fifty-two. Along João Pessoa, I walked around the Police Headquarters till I was outside the Violence Against Women Division, from where it was possible to track the movement of anyone who, through the gate for vehicles to come in and out, left the building, and who crossed Professor Freitas e Castro towards the employees' car park that was on the patch of land between Freitas e Castro and Leopoldo Bier. The activity around the women's division wasn't as frenetic as it was around the police jail on the opposite side of the building, but there was still plenty of movement, a moderate coming and going, especially of women accompanying other women, a not insubstantial amount of bustle. I called Andiara. She answered on the second ring. Hi, sorry to call you like this without sending a message first to see if you could talk, I said. It's OK, Actually I was thinking about you, she said. How're you doing, I asked. Funny, your gaúcho accent is more pronounced, You probably haven't even noticed, and she laughed, How am I doing, Well, I'm here, immersed in my reading, Realising how productive I am when you're not in Brasília, she said. That must be good, I teased. No, It's definitely not, I'd gladly swap a week of high productivity doing my reading here in my Brasília bunker for one night with you there in Porto Alegre, she said, and laughed again. Sounds like a fair exchange to me, I said. But tell me, How are you, she asked. I'm here in this place, this Porto Alegre, the whirring blender that is Porto Alegre, I said.

Thinking about me, she asked. I do think about you, I said. Then tell me more about you thinking about me, But first hold on a second, Let me just get out from under all these piles of paper, I'm in bed, Picture it, Under the air conditioner, covered in a bed sheet, which is covered in pieces of paper, stapled or loose or bound, and books, files, magazines, So I'm going to take advantage of the fact you called to get up, It's going to be my chance to give my back a stretch, I've been lying here more than three hours, An aparthotel bed, a bed that doesn't even come close to my lovely little bed up in the north, she said. I didn't mean to get you away from your reading, I said. Well you have now, And I'm incredibly grateful for it, Now I want to listen to you, You know you're going to have to talk to me a bit, don't you, she said. And we talked till, at a certain point, I asked if she found it very demanding dealing with the power that her role as federal prosecutor gave her. She said that given who I was, it was even possible I might know better than her what dealing with power was like. I explained that I was referring to the power of operating the machinery of the state. She laughed and said that, yes, they were indeed different kinds of power. I asked if, some-times, she didn't feel tempted to use her operational prerog-atives on certain people, more than she used them on some others. She asked if I was talking about making choices. I said I was talking about harassment. She said that the toughest thing, in some cases, was to leave subjectivity, prejudices and even small resentments outside, she said that for somebody from the Prosecution Service it wasn't usually as complicated as for a judge, who has the real power to decide people's fates, but that it would be cynical of her to deny that members of

157

the Prosecution Service did have huge power in their hands, particularly the prosecuting attorneys, which was no longer the case with her since she'd been promoted. I asked if she'd seen a lot of cases of reported harassment involving somebody in the police. Federal police, she asked. State, I replied. She asked me where I was going with this. I said I couldn't give any details. She said that if I couldn't give her any details, she wouldn't be able to help me in the way she'd like. I said it was a bit early to lay my cards on the table about certain matters, especially like this on the telephone. She laughed yet again and said she wasn't surprised I wasn't able to lay my cards on the table, she said I never laid my cards on the table a hundred per cent when it came to Porto Alegre and my Porto Alegre business, she was only surprised I couldn't say what I wanted down the phone. I laughed and straight away changed the subject. She was generous, allowing me to change the subject. We went on talking until I spotted Douglas coming out of the police building headed towards the car park. I checked the time on my phone. Nine-oh-five. I told Andiara I was going to have to hang up now and, without waiting for her to say what's up, I promised I'd call later or the next morning, sent her a kiss, hung up. I went up to Douglas, the Douglas who wasn't as young as the one in the Facebook profile photo. I said his name as he was just about to go into the car park. He turned and looked at me. You want to talk, Federico, he asked curtly. That's why I'm here, I said. He checked the time on his wristwatch. We can't talk here, Let's go over to my office, he said and crossed back over Freitas e Castro to the Police Headquarters building. He was already on the opposite kerb when I finished taking in what

I'd just done and what he had done in those couple of seconds and realised I needed to get moving. I picked up the pace so as to catch up with him. We went up to his office, the office of the head of the intelligence service of the Rio Grande do Sul civil police. He opened the door, turned on the light. Sit anywhere you like, he said, and I did, I sat on one of the six chairs around the conference table. He turned on the air conditioning, poured two glasses of mineral water from the mini fridge beside the office window, a window that looked out over João Pessoa, put one of them in front of me, kept the other. He went over to sit at his desk, which forced me to turn round. I want you to stop going after my niece, I said abruptly. Good to know that's the tone our conversation's going to take, Best for there not to be any bullshit, he said and took a sip of water. Only, before we deal with your niece, Federico Meira Smith, I want to know one thing, Where is your friend who killed my cousin with a shot in the chest, he asked. I stayed silent. You can go on and talk, I'm not recording, And don't tell me you don't know who I'm talking about, he said. Are you going to question me, I asked. No, this here's just a little chat I'm having in my office with a man whose work I know, I follow, I monitor, he said. Monitor, I asked. He nods. I get it, I said. I've been monitoring it for years, One time I even went along to a lecture of yours at PUC, the place was rammed so I just stayed at the back, People were applaud-ing you, You were giving them exactly what they wanted to hear about building a better world, and they were applauding you, A snake charmer, Skilful, very skilful, he said. I'm flat-tered, man, I'm really flattered to know you've been following my work, I said. I follow every step you take, Which isn't hard, since you're a celebrity, A human rights celebrity, a celebrity of hope, he mocked. You monitor my work waiting for me to screw up, I said while from a distance I examined the certificates, diplomas and honours of all kinds affixed to the walls of his office, everything from proof of his successful completion of a high-calibre guns course down to his graduation from Tae Kwon Do, Krav Maga and judo classes and his participation in various international intelligence-community seminars. I monitor, waiting, Just waiting, he replied. Look, Douglas, I'm going to tell you honestly, Really I don't know where Anísio's got to, I don't know where he ran off to, I haven't had any contact with him. You might not know, but your brother knows, Your brother and the other guys in your brother's crowd, I'm sure they know, he said. You're pressuring me, man, Is that's what's happening here, I asked. I want your friend, he said, Among the group that night, my cousin was the most naïve, the most guileless, the one who only ever wanted others' approval, to assert himself in front of the rest of us. Well, I'm guessing for a big old thug like him to have to launch himself onto a little guy along with three other thugs and on top of that using a knuckleduster yeah he really must have been oh such a poor little thing who really really needed to assert himself, I said. He looked at me with loathing. You know I don't think I'd have gone in for a career in the police if it hadn't been for that night, he said. Don't think I don't blame myself for not having prevented that fight that night, I said. My cousin's death could have been prevented if that attack by your crowd against mine hadn't happened, he said. It wasn't an attack, And we weren't the ones who started it, It was your friend, she started it, If you'd wanted to avoid trouble you'd have found a way to get her to say sorry to my cousin, You know what I'm saying, That's the problem with whites from the Porto Alegre élite, like you, You people never make way for anyone else, You guys are never wrong, Man, your people were totally wrong, your position and your attitudes were wrong, You were exercising the privilege of moneyed white folk to the hilt, Insisting we inadequate little people from the periphery stay invisible and put up with whatever we had to put up with from you, You know this, And you know that today, if somebody had been filming it on their cell phone, if there'd been witnesses prepared to talk, to go on the record about what happened, your friend would have been incriminated for using racial slurs, I said. She just made some stupid comment, the cop said, Those were different times, OK, She didn't physically hurt anybody, She didn't point a gun at anyone, She didn't kill anyone, he said. Fine, Douglas, Even though your friend was a jerk, I was the one in the wrong, I wasn't being rational, And I triggered the physical confrontation, Not her, And I know it doesn't make any difference telling you this now, but I want to tell you how bad I feel about your cousin's death, And I'm sorry I didn't listen when you asked me to calm down that night, I said. You know, Federico, it's been years since I gave up waiting for you to apologise, since I stopped needing your apology, he said. All the same, I do feel bad and I'm sorry, I said, and I got up and went over to him with my right hand held out for him to shake, but he didn't move, he kept both his hands on the top of his desk, though I kept on standing there with my hand out. We're OK, Federico, I've already put our argument outside the club behind me, he said.

But not the firing of that gun, and I sat down in the chair across the desk from him. It was murder, he stated, Just do what I asked you, Hand over your friend Anísio and, as far as the law allows, I'll try to make things easier for your niece, and those words returned our conversation to square one. You know, man, I said, I'm a cop's son. Sure, your father's a legend here, Douglas said. What I'm saying, I said, is that I know how to deal with the coldness of a cop, especially the less impulsive, more cerebral sort of cop, but I've got to tell you, this coldness of yours right now is like real psychopath behaviour, I said. He laughed. I laughed along to keep him company. Being a cop here in Rio Grande do Sul, in your father's time, that was one thing, Federico, but it's something else today, Besides, my role, my place in the big picture, it demands a different kind of restraint, I see it as restraint, what you think of as coldness, Because I deal with all kinds of insanity in this society, a society that doesn't value the police at all, you know, I'm the one conducting the orchestra, I'm used to neurosis, eccentricity, to people with suicidal tendencies, to people who truly are bad, I'm constantly dealing with bad guys, with real bad guys, bad guys from the streets and the bad guys I create myself, my subordinates who work undercover, infiltrating criminal organisations we're investigating, a number of them, actually the majority of them, neurotic themselves, with the same tendency towards self-destruction, police officers with screws loose, with bad thoughts in their heads, So don't you label me, because I've only ever done everything I could to not label you, he said. Man, just forget about my niece, I said. He took another sip of water, looked at me as if waiting for me to go back and take a sip of mine. You don't know who your niece is, Federico, You and your brother don't have the faintest idea what she's mixed up in, who she's mixed up with, You know I could have carried out the investigation completely on the quiet and not let the information that I'm after her leak out through the corridors here at Police Headquarters, But I wanted you and your brother to find out, precisely so that one of you would come to me, My money was always on you, Not because I wanted you to be the one who came here to beg, and he gave a subtle smile, but because I knew you were the one who'd be the least committed, emotionally speaking, the least affected by the girl's detention, and so the one who'd add two and two and find out it made four, And though I don't have the proof I'm after yet, I do have some solid clues, he said. Don't make shit up, man, I said, She's just a student who's well-informed, opinionated, wanting to fight for a society that's less fucked up than the one we've got, I said. I'm not questioning her good intentions, Douglas said, but rather the decisions she's been making and the company she's been keeping, and I'm telling you, they're no good, This generation doesn't have that nineteenth-century rhythm of ours, all that tiresome Hey you you're being exploited too, those little posters, those little protest marches, maybe they're less tentative, strategically, but they're also much more aggressive, amoral, too quick to waste time with party politics, their real war is online, there's no rest for them, they never get a break, It's a war of versions and inversions and subversions, of lies, when they take action it's the action of ripping the scalp off an enemy's head and displaying it on the internet for all the world to see, no matter the consequences, capturing virtual trophies and displaying them in their rankings, in the virtual clubhouse, accumulating likes the value of which most people of our generation can barely recognise, Your niece is smart, and I know you know she is, And, seeing as you've come at me with this business of coldness, I can tell you, she's a lot colder and more calculating than you imagine, he said. Man, you're sick, I said. Nothing of the sort, Federico, Nobody here's sick, What's going to happen to your niece is that we're going to lock her up and we're going to save her from herself, You can be sure that as soon as I've finished collecting the evidence to charge her, I'm going to charge her, her and her little friends, And there will be nowhere for them to run, By the way, did you know she has two computers, the one that's for show, whose IP my guys know better than the line-up of their own football team, and the other, which she uses to navigate the net anonymously, and which we know she has, but whose IP we haven't traced yet, he said. Why are you telling me this, I asked. Right, he said, Wow, I wonder why that might be, How about we say it's so that you give plenty of thought to how much I want you to hand Anísio over to me, And you can relax, If I've given you this information it's because your niece, even if you grab your phone right now and tell her everything I've just told you, won't have any way to cover her tracks, on the contrary, if she tries to hide them it'll only make things worse for her, she'll end up even more vulnerable and entangled, he said and got up, You should understand I'm giving you an alternative, to hand over Anísio, but beyond that there's not a lot you can do, And then there's also the matter of the gun, that's a whole other story, That MP service revolver, the gun she only brought to the protest because she'd agreed to lend it to a guy who ended up not showing at the protest, he said. Man, I'm going to break you, I said, and I stood back up. For your own good don't even think about it, he said, Calm down, Accept the fact that I got you, he said, That I've got you now and I'm going to get you every time you or your brother or your niece do anything stupid, he said. Look, man, if you want to be my enemy, I'm not going to be the one to stand in your way, I'll move to Porto Alegre, And then we'll get to run into each other all the time, I figure you're the kind of cop who likes cooking up a theory and then does everything possible to get hold of evidence to back that theory up, I said. So you'll come back to Porto Alegre after all these years, he said, impassive. Yeah, I'm going to move back home and make your life hell, Don't think you can intimidate me with your threats, You're not in charge of this city, You're not even in charge of the police, You're barely in charge of your own mental equilibrium, I said. He walked over to his office door, opened it. You can go, Federico, I'll be staying here a few more minutes, Finishing my mineral water, Thinking about what I'm going to do with the mineral water I poured you and that you rejected, he said. And without taking my eyes off him, I left the room, obliterated by the certainty that despite all the time that had passed, despite the two of us getting older, we'd learned almost nothing.

I leave my house through the garage door, my feet step onto the sidewalk, in my right hand the cotton sweater I decided to bring with me because the weathermen are predicting a sudden drop in temperature later this morning, in my left the plastic folder with the elastic fastening containing the documents and photos I'm going to need over the course of the day, and I walk up Coronel Vilagran Cabrita. On Bento Gonçalves I take a left away from the city centre, I go into Ki-pão, ask for one of their 'Cream Dream' cream puffs, pay, leave. I walk past the Partenon Tennis Club, it's impossible to ignore the tall grass begging to be cut, it's pretty much our neighbourhood's official social club but the guys still don't even bother taking care of the place. When I reach the State Savings Bank I cross the avenue at the pedestrian crossing, over the bus lane, I turn onto Tobias Barreto, go up to the first building on the right, I press the button for two hundred and two on the intercom, I wait. No one answers. I press again. Sleepy-voiced, Bárbara picks up. I've brought a certain something for you, I say. What sort of something, she asks. The Cream Dream from Ki-pão sort, I say. Listen, isn't it kind of early for a surprise visit, Oh Man of My Dreams, she says slyly, But I don't know, I wonder if I even want it, I'm just getting out the bath, I've got to finish a presentation for my experimental psychology class this afternoon, And it's a really complicated assignment, I'm just not happy with what I'm writing, she replies. I wait and she asks, A dream, you say, and I say, Nice and warm. Fine, Come up, and she buzzes me through the street gate and the internal door into the ground floor entrance hall. I go in, take the stairs. The apartment door is already open, the lukewarm air produced by her A/C drifting down the hallway, and there she is, standing in a short dress in light cotton, a dress that's red verging on pink contrasting with the indigenous complexion of her skin, a dress I don't know, which almost looks like a nightie. I hand over the parcel, give her a kiss on the cheek, head towards the sofa, toss my sweater down and then the plastic folder and then I sit next to the sweater and the plastic folder. She opens the packet, inhales the smell. And your mother, I ask. She's gone to help Aunt Alejandra, She's going to move again, Apparently this time she got into a fight with her resident building manager and his deputy, It took her less than a year after moving in this time, Honestly I don't know where my mother gets the patience, she says. Then, How are things going, putting her difficulty-level nine-out-of-ten question in front of all her level fives and below, the ones that as far as I'm concerned ought to be asked first to break the ice, really the glacier between us, what with her not having spoken to me on the four occasions I'd called in recent days, when I did end up getting through to someone it was her mother, a person who finds it incredibly hard to lie and who each one of those four times when I asked if her daughter was home ended up giving me every clue that Bárbara was indeed home and just didn't want to speak to me. Bárbara sits on the floor in front of the stand for the National Three in One Sound System, removes the dream I brought from its packet, takes a bite. God, I needed that and didn't even know it, Nobody in this world is better at guessing what I need in the morning than you, she says. I nod. I liked that little tape you made for me, she says by way of clarifying that she hasn't been avoiding me because of the K7 I left in the mailbox of her apartment a few days ago. You said you didn't want any more mixtapes, I say, provoking her a little. Your tapes always were your lowest blow, she says, You know that's why I asked you to stop, It almost makes me cry listening to those beautiful songs you find from who knows where, What were the first two on side B, she asks, and she relaxes a little. 'Musette and Drums' and 'Sugar Hiccup', Yeah, that English band is really good, I say. But I have to say, she said, I don't know if I like the way you didn't let the songs end, Oh, I really don't understand why you do that, why you didn't let them end, not a one, she says, questioningly. They do end, I say, They just don't end the way whoever made the record wanted them to end. If you ask me they don't end, and she offers me some of the dream. I contemplate telling her to listen again and pay attention to the lyrics right before the cuts, and to the way that, if she has the patience to put all those little pieces together, they form a complete and really desperate declaration of love, but I don't. I've already brushed my teeth, I say. All right, but what did you mean by cutting them all off practically halfway, Come on, You cut a couple of them off right near the beginning, she insists. You know that if I try to explain the reason I'll just be talking and talking and never give you a convincing explanation, I lie. She stares, it's her way of wielding the weapon of silence. Oh, I don't know, Bárbara, I falter, Seemed like the right thing to do at the time, Nothing wrong with a little novelty, I lie again. A little novelty, she says, You aren't the kind of person who does things for a little novelty, and she looks at me with those accusing eyes, the eyes of a Psychology student totally in love with her undergraduate programme. Making tapes for you, no matter how, that's what I like doing, I admit, avoiding the confrontation. She smiles. Come here then, Eat the dream with me, gesturing for me to sit by her on the floor. I'm OK here, I reply. You know I can't handle one of these dreams on my own, Come on, Just one bite and I won't pester you any more. I get up, sit down beside her, take the dream from her hand, put it on the tray on top of the stereo stand, try to kiss her mouth. She turns her face away. I lie back on the rug, bring my hand to the hem of her dress, pull it towards me, lift it a little more to reveal her thigh, she isn't wearing any panties, I turn onto my side, move closer, kiss her leg, slide the hem up her leg to her waist, she helps by raising her hips, I move on as far as her hair, she opens her legs, I continue until she opens them wider and my tongue reaches her pussy. She turns so that my mouth can fit better and I can lick her. I bring my hand to her breasts. Wait, she says, moving my hand away. I lick her clitoris, I suck, I bring my hand to the zip of my trousers to free my dick, I hold her waist again, I lick her until her body tenses up and the warm liquid spills from her into my mouth. She pulls away and stands up, she holds out her hand so that I can take it and get up too, she says it's time for me to go, all this has left her uneasy and even more confused than she already was. I get up, straighten my trousers, pick up the dream, take a bite, return it to the stand. The hardest part is not saying anything that matters, seeing as she isn't saying anything that matters either. We were so chatty and amusing, spontaneous and so connected, now we're two competitors in the game she invented when she broke up with me saying she was in love with a visual artist four years older than me, a kind of painting prodigy from the UFRGS Institute of Arts, one of several visual artists who did her portrait as a part of some art festival event at the Town Hall Free Studio, a game that truly came into its own when two months after dispensing with me she called me up saying she couldn't deal with how much she was missing me and couldn't deal with the confusion of liking two guys at the same time. I should have told her then it would be best to turn the page, each of us follow our own path, but I couldn't do it because I still liked her and because her rejection had hit me right in my pride, and I needed to recover somehow, I needed to fix it, cure it, my pride, my pride in what I am, pride in my capacity to learn, to grasp new things, pride in what my stature and my natural physical strength allow me to accomplish, pride in my tendency to position myself as leader and then to exercise that leadership, all of which were tested during my three years of high school with the Jesuits, where my parents sent me because when I turned fourteen I begged to be moved into a different school routine far away from Partenon, that Jesuit school still considered one of the best in Porto Alegre, where I ended up meeting her, Bárbara, whose family had emigrated from Colombia to Brazil in nineteen seventy-six, and who was in another class, but who, coincidentally, also lived in Partenon.

Yes, I desperately needed to rescue that pride that makes me who I am, and thereby counteract the damage done by my watching all the tenderness in me that made me care about her evaporate from one hour to the next, which is why I keep playing this game of hers, which is why I go on swallowing all her talk about just wanting to be honest about her feelings. I say she can call me any time she likes. She says she'll miss me, but that it'll be a while before she calls me again. Controlling myself, I say that missing somebody means nothing. She replies that missing somebody, sometimes, is the only trustworthy measurement that allows you to see what's really important. She's so different from the Bárbara I knew at the start of the year, so much more theatrical and so much more secure in her latest little cruelties that I don't have an answer for her. My emotional armour is falling to pieces now at an unparalleled speed. I just stand there watching her go to the door, open the door, turn to me, say thank you for the dream, Man of My Dreams, and smile. I head over to the sofa, pick up my sweater and the plastic folder with the elastic fastening, go to the door, which she makes a point of keeping wide open, I think of sliding past without touching her, but she pulls me over and kisses me on the mouth. I return the kiss. That mouth of yours, she says and sighs. You do that so much better than Adriano, You're so much more delicate, she announces with all the security of somebody certain of the impossibility of any more expressive reaction on my part. I force a smile and leave, go down the stairs telling myself that there's nothing more I could have hoped to get from that meeting than what she gave me. Down on the ground floor I meet the caretaker using a hose to water the building's flower beds and pots. He gives me a friendly greeting, without, however, sparing me his amiable Italian face projecting pity, almost distress onto me. Being a caretaker of the sort who interacts with all the residents, he undoubtedly knows there's an older guy who visits the girl in two-oh-two a lot more often than I do.

Back on Bento Gonçalves Avenue, I walk across the bus lane and set off on my way. On the corner with Barão do Amazonas, I pass the pool hall, which opens at 4 p.m. and only closes at ten the following morning, where, at this moment, a guy I know from the neighbourhood is playing games for money, for little sachets of cocaine, for doubles of Drury's whisky. I reach the corner of Paulino Azurenha, stop for a few seconds, look over towards the top of Maria Degolada Hill. If you're on this street you can't ignore it. I pass the main entrance to the São Pedro Psychiatric Hospital. I pass the São Jorge church, cross Salvador França, go to the main entrance of the Third Cavalry Regiment, the Osório Regiment. There are two soldiers standing in front of the door. Before I can say anything, one of them asks if I'm there for the selection. I confirm that I am. He asks to see my ID. I show it. He tells me to go in, explains how I get to the gym where I need to present myself. I thank him for the information, but my thank you is lost, he and his fellow soldier are already focused on the next guys arriving behind me.

At the door to the gymnasium, a trio of soldiers does a preliminary document check, one of them asks for my identity card and my certificate of military enlistment. I take my wallet from my pocket, open it, pull out the ID, hand it over, open the folder I've brought, hand over the certificate. This one's organised, he brought his CME in a nice little folder, That's the way to do it, You're the kind of recruit the army needs, says the one who's standing farthest from me. The one who's holding my documents looks me over and I look back. You want to serve, civilian, he asks seriously. I do, I lie. Do you want navy, air force or army, he asks. Army, I lie again. Go on in then, and good luck, he says, and he hands me back the certificate and my ID. I thank him and go into the gym without returning my certificate to the plastic folder, finding a couple of hundred guys waiting inside for the selection. I take a place in the snaking line, the line leads to eight tables where eight soldiers deal with each conscript individually. It takes nearly half an hour for my turn to come, but it does come. Good morning, conscript, says the soldier at the table, and he holds out his hand for my documents. I return his good morning, hand over the documents, he makes a note of my details on a form, repeats the question about which of the armed forces I want to serve in, I say it's the army, he asks if I've ever had any kind of serious accident, if I've ever fractured a bone, if I've ever had an operation, if I've ever had a venereal disease, if I've ever had any other of the diseases that he lists off, I answer the questions and when we finish he hands me the completed form and my documents, points towards the far end of the gym where other soldiers are organising groups of thirty candidates to go to the building where the medical department is, where the first part of the evaluation is to take place.

The medical department is a cavernous exercise hall. As soon as the last guy in the group is in and the soldier in charge shuts the door, I hear shouts of take off your shoes, take off your clothes, pile everything up in that corner, keep your pants on and nothing else, booming out of a sergeant standing next to two very grey-haired doctors, he's holding a short bullwhip, the kind for breaking in horses. I lead the way, the corner he pointed towards is on my side of the group. I take off my sneakers, my trousers, my T-shirt, I put the sweater and plastic folder on top of the pile and line up to be examined by the doctors. Over here, yells the sergeant, making it clear that giving orders by yelling is standard procedure for him, But before your evaluation by the doctors, I want to know one thing, I want to know because I'm sure that among thirty babies like you lot there's got to be one faggot, One pillow-biter, One fairy, I want to know who's the pansy, I'm going to count to ten, I'm going to give the shirt-lifter a chance not to serve, All he has to do is turn himself in now right now, I'm being serious, If the sissy-girl comes over here and tells me, in so many words, I don't want to serve because I'm a queer, sergeant, It's a promise, I'll let them go then and there, he says. Nobody steps forward. He walks down the new line that's formed, looking at each of us in turn. Very well, Let's pretend there are only real men here, he yells again, But if I catch one of you mincing about, eyeing some other conscript's pants, you're going to regret it, and he moves away from the line, stopping a little further ahead, turning back to face the group. You two there in front, you can step forward for your exam, he orders, and he stays where he is, observing everything with his arms crossed.

Having been one of the first to take off my clothes and position myself in line, I'm seventh to be seen, the doctor looks over my paperwork, says my name, That's me, I confirm. He looks at my groin, keeps his weary stare on my groin, I bring my two hands to the front of my pants, he tells me to lower them and then lift my scrotum, I obey, he tells me to pull up my pants, he takes my blood pressure while he listens to my heart, then tells me to breathe deeply three times while he sounds my lungs, he examines my throat, my eyes, my ears, makes notes on my enlistment form, says, with a weary voice that matches his weary gaze, that after the sergeant lets us out we're still going to have to go over to the next building for a battery of physical aptitude tests and that I can go. I leave the doctors' enclosure, really an open space demarcated by screens in a metal and cloth structure. The sergeant is still in the same place, motionless, his arms crossed. I walk over to join the others waiting for the last of us to be examined. As the minutes pass, some risk it, talk to one another, a few of the more daring even laugh, but it seems the sergeant doesn't care anyhow, his eyes remain fixed in the direction of the line of the conscripts the doctors haven't seen yet.

The last of us is done, the sergeant uncrosses his arms and comes over. Neither of the doctors emerges from their enclosure. I want you all looking at me now, I want you to form a circle around me, says the sergeant. Once the circle is complete, he goes back to shouting. I want all the blacks to take one step forward, he says. No one moves. Now, he says. Eleven guys do as they are told. I stay where I am. He leaves his position, walks around the circle taking a close look at each

175

of us. There are more blacks here, he says, If whoever needs to take a step forward doesn't do it now, all thirty of you are going to stay with me here in the barracks till six this evening, he threatens. Three other guys take a step forward. I stay put. He approaches the smallest of the three. No mirror at home, conscript, he asks, Got cataracts in your eyes, conscript, he asks, then yells, You're lighter than me, you piece of shit, Get back to your place. The guy takes a step back and can't help but flash a nervous smile. The sergeant breaks through the circle almost running down the two guys in his way, stops about three metres outside the circumference. I want those thirteen against that wall, And I want it now, he orders. The thirteen obey. I want you standing shoulder to shoulder, he orders. They obey. I want you to take off your underpants, he orders. They obey. I want you to stand on your underpants, he orders. They obey. Holding up the bullwhip, he walks over to the fifth from the right. Oh, how embarrassing, buddy, You really want to come in here with a dick that tiny, huh, and he stands in front of the kid, looking him in the eye, You trying to let down your race, conscript, he asks with a face almost touching the kid's. No answer, no reaction. I think I've found the fag, announces the sergeant back to our group, then asks the guy in question, Are you a fag, conscript. No, sir, sergeant, is the reply. Very well, conscript, Bet you've already been traumatised enough with a dick like that, I've seen clits bigger than that little cock of yours, Pick up your underpants and go join the others over there, he says. The kid bends down, picks up his pants, straightens up and comes towards us with tears running down his face. Let's keep moving, the sergeant shouts again, I want the twelve of you facing the wall, Noses touching the wall, he orders. They obey. I look over towards the doctors' enclosure, neither of the two is visible. Now I'm going to ask you, the sergeant resumes, Why is the world round, raising his voice to full volume when he reaches the word round. No one answers. I'm going to ask again, and if none of you answers me, all thirty will be staying till six tonight paying the price in sit-ups and cleaning latrines, and he looks over at us. And if one of you other assholes makes so much as a peep, in addition to the sit-ups and the latrines, you'll all be collecting horseshit by hand, out on the riding track, and he looks at his bullwhip. My head starts tingling, I don't remember my head ever having tingled before in my life. So what's it to be, he resumes, Those other guys aren't going to say a word, So what I want to know is why the world is round, No one leaves here till one of you twelve gives me an answer, he declares. What's with this lunatic, man, whispers one of the conscripts near me. The guy's a dirt-coloured Indian, Just because he's got that straight Indian hair he's pulling out the black kids to use as his punching bag, says another in an even lower whisper. Shut up, a third says, This thing's fucked-up enough already, don't make it worse, I don't want to be here till six o'clock because of you guys being reckless, he warns. It's already been two minutes, says the sergeant. Son of a bitch Indian, the nearest recruit whispers to me. I can't talk, I can't even look at that sergeant any more. The tingling in my head lessens when I stop looking at him and just stare straight down at the floor. I'll give you one more minute, And because I'm generous I'm going to give you a clue too, I'll give you the beginning of the answer, But I do think you're all heading for some punishment, Punishment for all thirty, he says vigorously. Neither of the doctors shows their face. Seems the guys in the group I'm in have finally understood that the sergeant is an actual and outright psychopath, so they've shut their faces once and for all, I can't even hear them breathe. The world is round so those blacks don't, the sergeant says, walking from one end of his little line-up to the other. Now I look up at him again. I'm waiting, The world is round so those blacks don't take a shit, he tries again, and as he passes by the second conscript from the left he strikes him lightly on his shoulder with the handle of the bullwhip, repeats the same phrase with the next conscript, saying, Time's up, Let's go, The world is round so those blacks don't, and he hits the next leg he passes with the bullwhip, not so lightly this time. Take a shit in the corners, whispers the guy next to me. The world is round so you fucking blacks don't, and he hits the shoulder of the fourth from the left, the tallest and fattest of the twelve, but the tall fat one turns around before I can blink and places a well-aimed punch in the face of the sergeant, who hits the floor.

I go out through the main gate of the barracks, I cross Salvador França, I stop outside the church of São Jorge, the door's open, I look inside. It's been four years since I've set foot inside a church. I climb the stairs, go in, position myself on the first bench. I put the plastic folder with the elastic fastening on the kneeler of the pew ahead, I sit down. I watch the altar, the unsettling light coming in through the stained-glass windows behind the altar. The tingling in my head starts again and soon spreads down my arms. The feeling of panic gets me to my feet. I breathe fast in the rhythm of somebody who's getting ready to take a deep dive, but without ever holding my breath. It wasn't the two conscripts being humiliated in front of the twelve dark black-skinned ones put up against the wall, it wasn't the two who were close to the one who threw the punch having held on to his arms not to restrain him but to support him, it wasn't the sergeant spread-eagled on the ground with a bloody nose, and it wasn't the doctor, the one who examined me, going out the door and returning with a lieutenant and another four soldiers, it wasn't the sergeant with the broken nose refusing any kind of help from the doctors and, having struggled to his feet alone, leaving the hall in silence, nor was it the lieutenant having asked for our attention to tell us that the mission of the Armed Forces is to make young people who serve our country stronger and tougher than they are already and that, as a result, those who are lucky enough to be selected might experience some psychological pressure from time to time, that it's all part of the learning process, nor was it how, before ordering us to put on our clothes and right after he notified us that he was going to accompany our group to the athletics area where the final physical tests would be taking place, he, the lieutenant, asked all of us quite calmly to keep what just occurred to ourselves, not to make too much of this most regrettable incident, and the group replied in unison yes, but I couldn't say yes, I couldn't even open my mouth, no, it wasn't any of that, what really wrecked me was the crying fit the tall fat one had straight after the sergeant's head hit the floor, the crying that revealed not his bravery but his despair, the despair of someone my own age who knew he'd ruined his life, ruined his whole life by not allowing himself to be humiliated, it was this crying that cast me down into a deep mental pit. I pick up my plastic folder, leave the church, walk down the stairs. I decide not to go to the centre of town to do the things I'd planned to do. I cross Bento Gonçalves, go into the snack bar on the corner with Aparício Borges, at the counter I ask for a bottle of Choco Milk. I breathe. I look at the three old men sitting at one of the tables, at the two ladies next to me at the counter, at the teenage couple who has just come in, at the two waiters, at the girl on the till, people from my neighbourhood, people who at some point in my adolescence I stopped seeing. I need to calm myself down, I think. I breathe. I take a couple of sips of the Choco Milk. I look out the window to the church and beyond that to the barracks. Calm, Federico, I think. I breathe, I calm myself, I slow myself down, and still I feel rage.

On Saturday, I woke up at seven fifteen, hung-over, with a hangover that wasn't thanks to the Steinhäger and beer I'd drunk at the Van Gogh restaurant to clear my head a little after coming back from Police Headquarters, and it wasn't thanks to my having called Bárbara when I reached my hotel to ask how the conversation with Roberta had gone, and her telling me the conversation with Roberta was weird, that the girl really did exude a disproportionate degree of self-confidence, which was hardly appropriate given everything that was happening, saying that the best thing would probably be for me and Lourenço to talk to her about that gun, and the sooner the better, because she, our Roberta, couldn't be treated like a child any more, and it wasn't a hangover caused by the physical exhaustion resulting from this sudden burst of recent activity after years of living such a sedentary lifestyle, it was the hangover of a man trying to adapt to his irreversible decision to leave Brasília and move back to Porto Alegre, a decision abruptly made manifest by way of his almost mechanical reaction to his confrontation with a police officer the previous night. And so, as the shower water came down, hot and bountiful, onto my head, I repeated out loud, pathetically, the exact words I'd said to Douglas about my moving to Porto Alegre and us running into each other. I stepped out of the tub, dried myself off, put on some clothes. I went downstairs to find a place to get coffee. I walked up Garibaldi, took Cristóvão Colombo, went as far as Doutor Barros Cassal, up to the corner with Independência, and into the Porto Alegre Bakery. I sat down at the counter, asked for a cup of coffee with milk and a roll, took out my phone, saw that during my walk a message had come in from Andiara, some good morning words accompanied by emojis. I waited for my order to arrive, put two sachets of cane sugar into my coffee with milk, picked up the little plastic stick, stirred, went back to the phone.

Sorry I couldn't talk properly yesterday, I wrote.

Hope everything's OK, she wrote back, and sent emojis.

All OK.

Any idea when yr back? Missing you, she wrote, and sent emojis.

Yeah, that's the thing.

That's the thing???

I'm going to stay in Porto Alegre another 3 weeks.

3 weeks? What about the commission? And your commitments here in Brasília?

I'm leaving the commission. The other things I can sort out from here. I can't see any other way.

Seriously? I'm devastated.

To tell you the truth, I'm no longer sure about Brasília.

Sure how?

About staying there.

Don't tell me you're thinking about leaving Brasília.

Yes.

Oh Lord. That's so strange. What's up?

Long story. I think I can only tell you what's happening in person, I wrote.

But you're OK, right?

Yeah, I'm OK, don't worry.

Missing you.

Missing you too.

I'll figure out a way to get to Porto Alegre if you don't mind.

Come.

Next week's going to be difficult but I'll organise things to come the following.

Yes, do come.

4 days in Porto Alegre, 3 nights, 4 days, sound all right?

As many days as you want.

I'm not pushing you, am I?

Don't worry, you're not pushing me.

Then I'm going to buy the tickets.

I'm glad.

She sent emojis. We'll talk later, she wrote.

Kisses, I wrote.

Kisses, she wrote, with more emojis.

Bárbara was where she said she'd be when, on the previous night, we agreed to meet in the Parque da Redenção, outside the chapel of the Divine Holy Spirit at the Municipal Emergency Hospital. In her left hand a jar of honey, in her right the handles of a cloth bag filled with fruit and vegetables bought at the Parque da Redenção's Eco-Market, a narrow corridor almost five hundred metres long made up of stalls from small rural producers from the Greater Porto Alegre area, stalls covered in tarps of various colours with gaps between them no more than two and a half metres wide for people to pass through, gaps through which people parade all their Saturday casualness as they hunt for organic products of various kinds and sources, a corridor that began a few metres from where she was standing. Hi, Am I late, I asked. No, Of course not, It's me who arrived early to do the weekly shopping, she said. Shall we go someplace else, I asked without hiding my happiness at being with her. How about a mint tea at Maomé, she suggested. Yeah, why not, I said. Oh, this is for you, and she held out the jar, It's grape-ivy honey, I bought it from a friend who's been making it for about fifteen years, It's a great natural detoxer, I'd recommend eating it with a spoon, and she handed it to me. Thank you, I said, Good, there's a lot, so I can share it with Lourenço and Roberta. She looked at me as if I hadn't understood what the present was really intended for. We went to the Maomé patisserie. We sat at the table by the door where it was possible to watch the comings and goings out on the sidewalk, we ordered tea with mint leaves. So, Federico, where do you want to start, she asked. We can start with Roberta, I said, Should I be worried about her, I asked. I think she's conflicted, probably a bit lost, and, of course, like anybody with more than two brain cells in their head in this ungoverned country, she's outraged, But there's something behind her outrage, There's an indifference that seems to be a way of stifling a feeling of fury, that's sort of risky and, I suspect, actually dangerous, But I don't know, it could be that head of hers has a slight tendency towards suicidal martyrdom, and there's a bit of obsession in there too, It's complex, it's hard to assess, Our meeting yesterday wasn't a session, Not in the traditional sense, It was just a conversation, a conversation that, as I made a point of clarifying to her, would not be confidential, A conversation that could lead to her being referred to another professional, There wasn't enough time for me to understand anything, really, Just enough for me to suspect, There are a lot of things going on in her head, in the head of the persona she's created for herself, It's a tough business, Seems like she and a good portion of her generation of young women have managed to attain a degree of understanding of the inequalities that we, our generation, well, I mean, That I, Even being plugged in like I am, That I can't reach without first going through dozens of theoretical formulations, she said. Should I be worried, I repeat. I think it's worth investing in a course of therapy, I do think this is a crucial moment for her, She's still impacted by the suffering of that friend of hers who lost her eye, But what happened to her friend wasn't the start of this state she's in, This refusal to accept things, Her rage, They were there already, Bárbara said. Rage, Could it really be, I asked. Rage, Refusal to accept, Terror, It's like she's terrified of the idea of not being able to be the lead actor in her own story, which reminded me of you, Though I don't know if it's so bad that she can't accept reality, that she might neglect the risks posed by reality, The difference between the two of you is that she hasn't been knocked down yet, not really, Even with everything that happened to her on Wednesday, she hasn't been knocked down yet, Maybe she's stronger than you, she said. No doubt at all she's stronger than me, I said. But it's only a matter of time, Life's going to knock her down soon enough, I'm quite sure of that, And it's going to knock her down hard, Being the way she is, You can count on it, it's a matter of time, Which is why I think it's important to prepare her, she said. The waiter brought us our tea in a spherical ceramic pot.

When she'd paid our bill at the patisserie, Bárbara suggested we walk over to the Parque da Redenção's central fountain. I offered to carry her bag. We went off down José Bonifácio towards the Monument to the Expeditionary. And what about us, Dreamboat, she asked me, once more living up to her role as the one always willing to initiate whatever conversations the other person didn't have the nerve to start up. You're in a relationship with a cool guy, What can I say that would make any sense faced with a situation like that, I said. We can't seem to disconnect from each other, Isn't that right, she said. We have our love, I said. Our love and our friendship, And that's beautiful, but I know you're kidding yourself, as you've done so many times before, imagining it would be good if we got close again, if we tried again, Am I wrong, she asked. I don't know, Bárbara, Maybe it's one of those crises, something to do with turning fifty, I said. I think you can do a lot better than that, she said, You always talk about my love for you but it was your love for me that made me stronger when I needed it, Federico, It was the way you always took care of me that pulled me out of the fixes my crazy head got me into, You're the one who never gives up, And that's wonderful, Maybe it's me who's not up to that passion of yours, that suffering over us that you decided was a precious thing, a thing that could nourish you, Because I've tried, You know I have, And you know it didn't work, she said. I'm better now, I said. Listen, she said, Because I love you more than I've ever loved any other guy, but our time has passed, Back there I lost you and you won me back, And it was incredible, despite the pain, But don't you get the sense that if we try again it's just going to look pretty dumb on our part, she wondered. I didn't answer. We're close to one another, and we always will be, And from time to time you're going to get yourself in trouble and you'll look me up, she said. And propose marriage, I said. She laughed. And it'll be good, she said. It will, I said. Because we, you and I, in this distance and closeness of ours, we're always going to be desperate, she said, and took my hand. I really would have liked for us to work out, I said, restraining myself faced with the distressing naturalness of this confirmation of a love that would never be repaired. But we did work out, Federico, It's a cliché, but we did work out in the end, We're here, now, holding hands, We have our friendship, our integrity, our love, and she made me put the bag down on the ground, and made me smile, and kissed me.

After we said goodbye, dismantled by Bárbara's sweet and violent way of telling me that she didn't feel up to suffering again at my hands, at least not enough to embark on a new attempt to rebuild our relationship, our intimacy, our fierce happiness as she described it at one point during one of our good periods, a relationship that had already given all it had to give, I walked from the Parque da Redenção to my parents' house in Partenon, where I was to have lunch with them, Lourenço and Roberta.

187

It wasn't easy to put the key into that door and walk into that front yard. I knew that my father, austere as only he could be, would not refrain from bombarding me with questions about Roberta's behaviour, about the gun, about what I'd done to help Lourenço and what I'd also failed to do. I was lucky, Lourenço arrived before me, and so by the time I arrived the all-powerful father had already grilled the son he always went easier on. In theory, the old man wouldn't be so inclined to eat me alive.

They were already at the table. Roberta with her head lowered, evincing no sign of any tendency towards martyrdom, obsession, a refusal to accept reality, any rage or terror, none of the things Bárbara had suggested. After the usual family greetings my mother called me to help her carry the two serving dishes to the table, the one with cod and potato and the one with white rice with walnut, and also the two big bowls, the one with the green salad and the one with the mixed salad. Before having lunch we said the Our Father holding hands. My father, ardent Catholic that he had become with the passing of the years, opened an eye from time to time to check whether Roberta and I were at least moving our lips, since he knew I only ever recited the Lord's Prayer when I was with my parents, at their request. Lourenço, Roberta and I waited for my parents to serve themselves and then we served ourselves in turn. My mother must have indoctrinated my father, because he restrained himself. He wanted to know about the weather in Brasília, he wanted to know how the Grêmio Náutico União basketball team were doing in the state and national rankings, and at no point did he address

Roberta. When we finished lunch, Roberta said she was going to the living room to watch a bit of TV, everybody exchanged glances, we knew she hated TV, but nobody made any comment. My mother asked her to shut the hallway door so the sound from the living room wouldn't spill into the lunch room. Roberta obeyed. My father glared at us, said he didn't want to know about the gun, didn't want to know where the kid, as he usually called Roberta, had found the thing, if the official version of how she'd ended up carrying the revolver had been constructed with expert advice from the lawyer, he wasn't going to be the one to change her story, but he said he wanted to know what the two of us had to say about Roberta being mixed up with acts of terrorism. My brother and I exchanged a glance. And Lourenço said there was no possibility of his daughter having committed any act that could be linked to terrorism, he said he'd been doing some research and was getting a better understanding of why these loopholes had been left in Brazilian antiterrorism law, bills passed months before the new government took power, leaving room for interpretations that allowed the law to be used to criminalise social movements and restrict social activity, he said he could even conceive of what margin there might be for somebody, in some way, to try to use it, maliciously, as a basis for getting Roberta into deeper shit, but he said that he knew his daughter and he knew she was only interested in protesting against injustice, and he looked to me and then our mother. Then, taking me by surprise, and Lourenço even more, my father asked what we had to say about Deputy Director Douglas Pederiva Setúbal. We were too stunned to reply. Federico, my father said, looking straight through me in that way only my father could. What, Dad, I asked. Say what you have to say, he said. How did you know, I asked. I've still got my connections in the police, I've got my eyes and ears on the force, Not in the precincts so much, Or anyway only in a few of them, But at Headquarters and in the Police Academy, and he smiled candidly, with a candour that would never have been in his face thirty years earlier, There I've still got quite a few eyes and ears in case I ever need them, my father said. For a change, I have no idea what the two of you are talking about, Lourenço exclaimed. I thought it best to give him an explanation. Yesterday, after I left your place, Lô, I went to the Police Headquarters to talk to this Douglas guy, I went to ask what he wanted with Roberta, because, doing a quick Google search of his name, I realised he was an old acquaintance of mine, I said, omitting any reference to the fight outside the Leopoldina in nineteen eighty-four, information that would be too much for my father's brain. He's a guy who's been carrying a grudge against me and who might want to take his hatred out on Roberta, I said. That's a new piece of information, my father said. What happened between you two, Lourenço asked. Not worth going into detail, I said. I also figured that talking about the fight at the Leopoldina would also be invoking the memory of the gun, which wasn't worth it. This fellow is pretty confident, from what I've been able to pick up, my father said. Don't worry about him, Dad, I said, I'm going to come back to Porto Alegre and. You're going to come back to Porto Alegre, my mother, who was following the conversation in strategic silence, interrupted me. Yes, Mum, Yes I'm moving back, I said. That's great, son, my father said. I swear I'm only hearing this now myself, my brother said, looking at the two of them with a Don't blame me expression. But to get back to this detective person, said my father, who wasn't about to lose the thread of the conversation, The problem with these guys just joining the force who think they run the show is that they become blind with regard to some of the rules of the game and underestimate those of us who appear to have left the stage, He might try to ruin Roberta's life and think he's untouchable and all that, but the two of you know, and my father didn't look at us as he said this, he looked at our mother, It's hard to find anybody in the police who doesn't secretly have feet of clay. My brother and I just stared at him, rather astonished at this, because, over the years, our father, who had become a full-time businessman, had given the impression of having lost his policeman's hot-headedness, but it seemed not. He's from Moinhos de Vento, And that's already enough for us to guess at what's coming down the track, I said. There's always some difference between an officer from a poor background and an officer from a rich background, my father said, surprising me again, The tycoons can't shake that arrogance they have, that overconfidence, it's something inherent in their class, he said. Once in the VIP area, always in the VIP area, Lourenço said. It might sound strange my saying this, but I learned a lot more about rich people, and especially about rich white people, when I was devoting myself to private security, installing and managing video surveillance systems, organising security escorts, private protection, things our brothers generally can't pay for, than I did in the police, my father admitted. I can imagine, Lourenço said. Surprised at my father having differentiated between blacks and whites, a rare occurrence indeed, I preferred to say nothing. The fear that the rich whites and upper-middle-class whites feel when a black man is captured on the cameras we've installed knocking at the doors of their houses is indescribable, Even if it's at midday, even if the black man is well dressed, It makes no difference, They go into a panic, If there's one thing this firm of mine teaches me every day it's that the rich are getting more and more worried, more and more cowardly and, as a result, they behave worse and worse, That the group of people who think black men and women are disgusting is only growing, That the racism in the heads of these rich people is something that isn't going to end any time soon, Naïve of anyone to think the contrary, and here he was addressing me, And so, maybe not even because of racism itself, but because of the advantages a person has if they come from where they come from, we can expect total arrogance, total arrogance just to begin with, on the part of this particular officer, my father said. You think so, Father, asked Lourenço. I'm rarely wrong, son, my father said. When I move back here I'm going to make his life hell, I said. All right, Federico, And I'm not going to say you shouldn't, my father said, But this Douglas fellow is going to run aground all by himself, I can feel that in the air, Even without my ever meeting the man I can sense it's going to happen, my father said. I don't want him just to fuck up on his own, Dad, I want to fuck him over myself, And it's going to be out in the open, it's going to be all legal and above board, A public denunciation of the way he operates in that little Intelligence and Strategic Affairs division of his, I said. My father sighed, looked at my mother, looked at my brother, said nothing. I glanced over to the door to the hallway that led to the living room, to double-check that it was indeed shut, and then moved closer to the three of them. Douglas told me there's compelling evidence against Roberta, I whispered. That's something we're going to have to find out for ourselves in the coming days, my father said, My work in forensics has always made me suspect and expect the worst of other people, even people I knew and, sometimes, people I liked, since I've occasionally caught close colleagues trying to suppress, alter or adulterate evidence. But I can't imagine anything bad coming from Roberta, On the contrary, if my granddaughter has the courage to fight for other people she can't, as you've said, be one of the bad, What the military police did emptying out that building was inhuman, he stressed. And, controlling myself so as not to exacerbate my niece's situation, since all of us around that table, even if we might have looked like we were holding firm, were still pretty shaken by everything that had happened, I couldn't help but notice in those words of my father's an indisputable recognition of the efforts of one citizen devoting herself to defending the rights of others. Leave Roberta here with us, Lô, Leave her here, let me talk to her, my mother said. It's not going to be easy, Mum, Lourenço said. It's true, Mum, I said. Go out, the two of you, referring to me and Lourenço, Go get a beer someplace, After clearing the table your father will go to his study to distract himself on the internet, And I'll get the drawings I've been picking out for the next exhibition, I'll go into the living room to show her and I'll talk to her there, it'll be no trouble at all, my mother announced, getting up, and leaving no doubt that our family lunch was over.

We went to the Baden Café on the corner of Jerônimo de Ornelas and Vieira de Castro, we sat outside, with a view of John Paul I Square. We ordered two espressos. I told Lourenço who the officer going after his daughter really was, I told him some details of the conversation I'd had with Douglas. Lourenço got quite uncomfortable when I explained that his condition for not coming down hard on Roberta was us handing over Anísio's head on a platter, he said a cretin like that had to be the worst kind of cop, the kind of flunky who was more worried about protecting a bank window than the life and dignity of somebody who's in the shit and trying to get out of the shit. Even with every justification, that comment sounded strange to me, because Lourenço, though he flirts with the underworld of our neighbourhood much more than I ever did, and is far better protected against our father's usual stoicism, wasn't in the habit of speaking ill of police officers, speaking ill of the police, not openly, not emphatically. He asked more about Douglas. After his questions and my answers came to an end, I asked if he could tell me where Anísio was. He said he wasn't sure looking for Anísio was a good idea. I insisted. He said he needed to think. I respected that, I didn't ask any further questions about his friend. We ordered a craft beer. We talked about how crazy my return to Porto Alegre was going to be, the hassle of looking for an apartment to rent, sorting things out for the move, going through all the bureaucratic bullshit to transfer the headquarters of my NGO. I told him that during the lunch at our parents' the idea had occurred to me of starting up a project with Roberta, a project geared towards the promotion of research into techniques for rescuing black youths as well as providing courses on the political history of black culture in Brazil and also staging political training activities aimed at black youth in the city's eastern zone, putting Roberta in place to manage it. Lourenço said he'd be very grateful if I would give his daughter that opportunity, he said she'd benefit a lot from an opportunity like that. I said if there was anyone who'd benefit it was me, I said it was quite possible Brasília was no longer doing me much good, that I was feeling weird there anyway, that coming to Porto Alegre to face this whole situation had helped me understand how out of place I was in so-called real life, I admitted how brutal I was finding it looking back and seeing how little difference everything I'd done had made, that, overall, after my nearly fifty years, I was starting to resent the sturdiness of my mediocrity, my inability, despite years of activism, to have created a single enlightened, salvational idea, a single idea that was truly transformational, starting to see that I'd been spinning around the necessary-obvious, basically treading water, as my father used to say. Lourenço told me I was being a very convincing drama queen, that the statuette would be in the post in a fortnight, and he laughed, then he said it was inevitable that one day awareness of everything would come, he said I shouldn't think so much, and that age must have taught me by now that sometimes the best thing was not to dwell on stuff too much. I said my radar no longer picked up certain things, certain behaviours, certain conflicts, I said I was losing my touch. He laughed, he said losing a few illusions about ourselves was a part of the ride, that I should just accept it. I said when I grew up I wanted to be just like him, to learn how to copy this foolproof serenity shit of his. He laughed and said for something like that to happen I would have to be born again.

The waiter brought a second bottle of beer. Remember that time you insisted I go with you to that meeting with some of the leadership of the black movement who wanted to sue that radio announcer from here in Porto Alegre, that guy who told a racist joke on-air about that federal deputy from the workers' party in Rio de Janeiro, calling her a monkey, Lourenço asked. I do, of course, it was right after the elections, If it hadn't been for that little lawyer from the city council having persuaded the majority of them to drop the lawsuit and go for a campaign to boycott the radio station instead, that moron would have been convicted and possibly out of work to this day, I said. Well then, 'derico, during that meeting, I was looking at those people and asking myself why, unlike you, I felt I had no connection at all to their attitude, to their cause, to their lives, to their truths, I was thinking, since that was the first time I took part in one of those meetings, that those people's war, all the fizzing excitement of their speech, had nothing to do with me, Lourenço said. They installed an app in me that they didn't install in you, I teased while I poured beer into his glass and then into mine. Or the other way around, he retorted. I laughed. You know, Federico, this summer I took a five-day course on genetics and sports performance, and in the course there was this module on epigenetics and epigenetic inheritance, it's an area that has to do with the transmission of experiences from parents or grandparents down to their children or grandchildren, A transmission that doesn't happen through DNA but by some methods only peripheral to DNA, methods that science is still investigating, he said. It's like when somebody's parents have been subjected to some kind of inhuman treatment, they produce children with an inborn, extreme fear of whatever bears any relation to that inhuman treatment, So sounds, objects, colours, smells, Is that it, I asked. Yeah, that's more or less it, Lourenço said. So what, I asked. So I think if that's true, if you think about it, you must have inherited some kind of pain from our enslaved ancestors, A kind of pain I never inherited, he said. Dunno, I said. You've got that need to mark out your territory the whole time, And that stresses you out, My vision of life is different, My weapons are different, I don't pay the least bit of mind to the racists who cross my path, he said. I've never had that ability, I said. You've always needed to get the upper hand, Wherever you were, you always needed to dominate, It's just in your nature, bro, It's like this innate need, he joked. That's harsh, I said, but I was laughing now. Hardly, he said, laughing too. It was good to see him relaxed. I've had my ambitions, it's true, You had yours, Everyone does, I said. I understand, he said. For real, I don't think I have any more big projects in me, any more big plans, I said. That's the question, he said, You've always been one for big projects. And besides, I said, I've been getting the feeling that the era of big actions, of big campaigns, is over. Yeah, seems like the next few years aren't going to be very friendly towards big projects, towards big altruistic interventions here in Brazil, This crisis is hitting real hard, he said. There's an end of a cycle on its way, I said. For you it's got to be complicated accepting that, he said. I said nothing. It wasn't good before, It's not good now, right, he asked. For several seconds I just stared at my glass of beer, then I made a comment about how good the beer was. And he agreed, nodding.

Lourenço left me on Felipe Camarão, at the Lipe Bar, where I told him that, if I was lucky enough to find a table on the sidewalk, I was going to stop off for two or three quick ones for the road which, at around eight, eight thirty, would probably kick-start my system at least enough to get back to my hotel on foot, throw myself onto the bed, and then finally shut down once and for all and refuse to leave my room again till Monday. There were two tables free. I sat at one of them, asked for a six-hundred mil Original, took out my phone, opened WhatsApp, sent a message to Micheliny saying I needed to talk to her first thing on Monday and that, if she didn't have time for me then, to tell me when would be the best time to call. I finished my beers in under fifteen minutes, that's the problem with drinking alone, I drink too fast.

Not twenty minutes after I sent the message, Micheliny called me. Can you talk, she asked. I can, can you, I asked. I can, she said, I was a bit concerned at that request of yours to talk first thing on Monday, So I decided to call, Can I help, she asked. I'm leaving the commission, Micheliny, I'm really sorry, But I've got some serious things to deal with here in Porto Alegre, I'm going to have to stay on around here for a few more weeks, And I know I won't be able to dedicate myself to the commission the way you and the others expect me to, I said. What can I say to news like that, she asked, I'm really sorry to hear it, Federico, In a way, you're the most experienced member of the team, The commission will lose a great deal if you go, and that's the truth, she said. To a lot of people this commission is a big white elephant, Micheliny, I said, an initiative that's doomed to fail, But all the same I'm still a bit hopeful, And I know you won't let them use our work to undermine the policy of racial quotas in education, I did get a chance to see that you've had a solid political education, I don't know in which direction the reading you've done in the past has taken you, And that doesn't matter to me anyway, But I know the fact of you being a career public functionary at the ministry and filling the position of aide answering directly to the ministers in the new government doesn't mean you've bought into all the new government's plans, I'm a sceptic, a malcontent, but I've never lost my ability to spot and root for whoever shows some real concern and who, even in adversity, devotes themself to the people in the greatest need, I can still root for people like you, people who confront what needs to be confronted, I said, being a little condescending but unable to find another way of talking to her that wasn't likewise going to lead me down a path where there would be some condescension. Good to hear that, she said. The truth is, the commission did end up surprising me, I said. Me too, she said, Ever since I came to Brasília, after I passed the public exam in twenty ten, I never gave any thought to certain questions, I gave up my militancy, gave up my agitating on behalf of racial equality, which began during my time in college, because at a certain point I realised there were a lot of black people who weren't even helping themselves, who didn't want to see and didn't want change, I realised how frustrating it was to keep arguing for someone who didn't want to help himself, and I gave up the struggle even though I knew that this business of not helping themselves wasn't exactly right, and I went off to get on with my life, The commission helped me to rescue some of my thinking, It made me re-establish some personal connections that had been neglected, It even encouraged me to stop straightening my hair, My 4C-type hair, And it also reduced my chronic guilt a little, that omnipresent guilt, the guilt that I have and that, I think, all the dark black people like me in this country end up having, even if they don't talk about it, Like I read somewhere once, an uncontrollable shame about themselves, a fracturing, The commission and the people on the commission have helped me go back to reflecting on my identity, And I'm grateful to everyone for that, she said, The day to day of public service alienates us so violently that it makes us cowards, she said. I mean to write a paper analysing the commission's role, putting forward a few proposals, And I hope you'll allow me to do that, I said, interrupting her epiphany. A paper, she asked. Yes, a paper of about ten pages at most, I said. I'm sure it'd be a significant contribution, I'll do what I can to make use of it on the commission, she said. Thank you, I said. By the way, I want to put that proposal of yours up for discussion about embedding monthly or twice-monthly reflections on slavery and the indigenous holocaust into school calendars, That's one of the initiatives we can, I think, argue for, And I think, like you said, the commission is going to fail, but not in the way some people might be hoping, she said. That's what I'm rooting for, I said, That the commission doesn't fail in the way the agents of evil hope it will, I said, and laughed. I know how much some of the bosses are rooting for me to fail as the coordinator of our working group, Micheliny said. Black people can't make mistakes, I said. That's what they say, she said, and laughed.

I was on my fourth beer when, in the middle of reading some messages in my WhatsApp groups, I got a message from Ruy, the Ruy from the commission. He wanted to know how I was, he said Micheliny had just informed him that I was going to leave the commission, he asked me to reconsider, assured me he could work out some way of me taking part over the internet, he said he believed the two of us could still get a lot done, do some good work, we as the two oldest in the group, he said it would be a pleasure to talk to me before Monday, asked me to give him a chance to convince me. Then, perhaps sensing that, once I had read his message, I wasn't going to respond, he sent nothing else.

I shouldn't have ordered the fifth beer, but I did.

Sitting at that bar table, exposed to the electricity of night-time in Bom Fim, the sharp familiarity of Bom Fim, alone, I felt the weight of the first day of my definitive return to Porto Alegre. Unsure of my ability to add anything to what I'd already said to Andiara that morning, something that went beyond the affective barrier between us that I still hadn't removed, but which I should have removed, I called her, asked her to come as soon as she could. And she said she had just bought her ticket to Porto Alegre for nine days later, she said she was happy and she said she felt love for me.

Ten p.m. The sixth beer on my table sat there almost untouched. Lourenço appeared in front of me, he said he'd gone to my hotel and that, on being informed at reception that I hadn't got back yet, he came right back to the Lipe Bar to see whether I, the city's newest displaced inhabitant, was still there knocking back beer after beer, battering my liver, anaesthetising my soul. That arrival of his, the way in which he arrived, irritated me a bit. I asked why he hadn't called first. He asked the waiter for a glass and sat down, he said he'd decided to take me to Anísio, that Roberta was going with us, that he'd told her everything, that she needed to know about the gun, that if she wanted to be an adult he wouldn't be the one to stop her becoming an adult. I said I needed to see Anísio too, that it wasn't in order to turn him in, I just wanted to see his face, I wanted to try to figure out some way of putting what had happened that night behind us. Lourenço said he knew what I wanted, he said he was on my side, he gave my shoulder a little pat and explained that he hadn't called because he wasn't keen on giving the police officer any new opportunities, that if the man really knew what he was doing there was no guarantee our phones weren't already being tapped, monitored, he said that he'd been to Augusto's house to ask if there was any chance of our being followed by the civil police or picked up by public security cameras, and that he, Augusto, had assured him that, with the police force dealing with a budgetary crisis like the one Rio Grande do Sul was experiencing, there wasn't the slightest possibility of that happening, that however obsessed with us this man might be, he wouldn't be able to get hold of the resources to mobilise a team to follow us twenty-four hours a day, but he explained that the danger was cell phones and computers, but most of all cell phones, that tapping and monitoring cell phones wasn't especially tricky or expensive, and so if I really wanted him, Lourenço, to take me to Anísio, I would have to leave my cell phone behind, along with his and Roberta's, back at his house, which was where we were going after finishing my last beer, after picking up my things at the hotel and checking out, because, from that night on, I'd be staying at his place, and he said we'd be hitting the road to Anísio before 8 a.m. I asked how we'd do it without phones, He said he'd just bought a pre-pay and a chip at the mall in case of emergency, that he'd leave the number with our mother, that there was no way our mother's phone was being tapped too. I thought it best not to insist, not to question that excess of caution. He finished my bottle of beer on his own. I thought about what Bárbara had said to me, not once but many times, about my finding it hard to see any defects in my brother, I thought the moment might have come for me to do some growing up as far as our relationship went, time for me to mature inside our invisible impervious glass bubble, maybe the time had come for me to learn to see him as someone apart from my great crusades, indeed to remove him from the context of my crusades altogether. When he finished, I got up. I paid the bill, and by the time I was back on the sidewalk he'd already pulled the van up outside.

He drops his holdall onto the table in a way that does nothing to avoid the sharp thud against the wooden surface thanks to the .44 short-barrel revolver that's inside it, he asks if what I'm drinking is filter coffee or Nescafé. I reply it's a proper Diana made in the electric coffee maker. He wants to know if there's plenty more. I say yes and that it's come out nice and strong too, the way he likes it. He hangs his jacket on the back of the chair next to the chair where I'm sitting, gives me a then I'll hitch a ride on your coffee and heads to the kitchen to help himself. You got in late last night, I call so as to be sure he hears me. Two in the morning, he replies. Something big, I ask. Four dead in a single incident, he replies. Four dead, you mean like a massacre, I ask. From the kitchen there comes no reply, just the opening and closing of the cupboard doors. He comes back in carrying his favourite mug filled to the brim and a plate with a pile of Isabela cream crackers, puts the mug and plate down near the bag, doesn't sit down. Four bodies tied with telephone wire to chairs just like these ones we have here at home, Four shots from a .38, one shot in the back of each neck, In other words, Execution, he says. You already know who the four are, I ask. Yes, Two of Sapucaia's drug kingpins, one of the guys' little hookers and a mid-ranking police officer, a veteran from the São Leopoldo station, who, as far as anyone knows, was an honest guy, he says, and he sits on the opposite side of the table, pulls his plate and mug nearer, looking at me the way he has a habit of looking at me when we're talking without my mother or my brother around, the same way that, eight years earlier, two weeks after CRT installed the long-expected phone line in our house, he said something to me like, Federico, as of today, whenever the phone rings, before the maids and the cleaners and before your brother and your mother, you're the one who's going to answer, then he waited for me, at the ripe old age of nine, to process his command before detailing what, precisely, I was to answer, how I was to answer, and then laying out the reasons why, explaining that a police forensics expert who takes part in interrogations, inquiries, who carries a gun and testifies at arraignments, at jury trials, who doesn't hide behind paperwork, is as hated and under threat from lowlifes as any other of his fellow police officers who aren't afraid to show their faces. And, in the years following that conversation, there were indeed three occasions I answered the telephone and heard strange voices on the other end of the line threatening our family, asking if I was Federico or Lourenço, saying they knew where our school was and asking me to tell my father it wouldn't be any problem for them to pick us up after class and take us for a ride. Where were the bodies found, I ask. In a shed at the back of an abandoned plot in the rural part of Esteio, he says. And what are the chances of finding out who did it, I ask. We've already got two suspects, And a team out to catch them, and then, with great caution, but without asking permission, he takes the newspaper from my hands, pulls out the crime pages and hands me back the rest. No way you kill an officer from the civils and get away with it, Right, I say provocatively. There are just some rules that can't not be followed, he replies. Rules with no exceptions, and I'm waiting for him to reply or, as he commonly does, to assert it doesn't matter whether a cop who looks crooked made a mistake or is just plain guilty, that finding the perpetrators is what matters to the force as a whole. But he doesn't reply, he just gives me his categorical we're going to sort it all out today, it won't drag on past today, he takes two sips of his coffee and focuses on the news in the crime section. His determination, every bit as great as his concern not to make any mistakes, is something I find inaccessible, unattainable, like his rage, a rage that's kind of like this superpower, a kind of high-octane fuel that never runs out. Where he gets this rage from, that's a question I never stop asking myself. When he finishes his coffee, having already concluded his reading of the paper, he asks if today isn't the day I present myself for the selection for military service. I nod, point at the plastic folder with the elastic fastening on the top of the sideboard behind him, I say that inside I've got my certificate of enlistment and that I'm going to present myself at the barracks at nine. He takes the last cracker on the plate, breaks it in half, says he's rooting for me, stresses that serving is a unique opportunity for a young lad to understand himself, to mature, to become a real man. I say sure, living the life of one of those military types for a year is totally going to help me to understand myself better. Without picking up on my irony, he says that spending time with people sneakier and smarter than me would be a good experience for me, it'd give me more confidence. I don't want anything to do with those military guys, Dad, I say in a tone that is discordant with my usual when talking to him. Ours is a government of soldiers, Federico, The General-President is the man in charge in Brazil, It's foolishness to underestimate their power, And then there's the CPOR officer training, An officer is always an officer, doesn't matter if he's in the reserves, You can make contacts there, get access to privileged information, learn how things work, And I don't need to tell you nothing happens in this country unless the military want it to, Nothing happens unless it happens their way, and he brings one of the halves of the cracker to his mouth. I want to keep far away from their way, Dad, and I gesture quotemarks with my fingers when I say their way. You're just like your mother, you have trouble dealing with reality, You think it's best to steer clear of it, The world isn't the way you two think it should be, Federico, But it's no use turning your back on reality, I'm sorry to tell you, he says. One day the military is going to leave, you know they will, and I hope with all my strength they're going to pay for all the bad things they've done and are still doing, and as I listen to my father I try to control myself because I know that he's being unusually tolerant of my aggressiveness. You've still got all those ideas from your high school teachers in your head, It's time to grow up now, Time to start thinking about putting theory to one side a bit, Don't be drawn off course by the sirens' song, he says. I think of throwing in his face the fact that, being in the civil police, he has to obey the orders of those same soldiers, orders that come through the mouths of his superiors at the civil police HQ but which, in reality, are orders from the military, that he's part of the whole machine that, belatedly, I, along with most of the adolescents of my generation, am starting to understand and starting to despise, I think, but I don't do it, I don't play that game, I don't talk, it would be a mistake on my part, an inexcusable act of cowardice. You believe in Father Christmas, son, That troubles me, he concludes. Listen, Dad, I say, laying my cards on the table, gearing up to the confrontation he's asked for, Last week I called your friend Damásio, and I asked if he had space in his schedule to see me at Southern Military Command headquarters because I needed to ask his advice and, if possible, for his help, And two days later I went to his office, He received me there, pretty pleasant like always, And I told him about how I'm in the middle of my second semester of university, And I said serving in the army was important, but that it was going to delay my studies, And I asked if there was any way he could prevent my being selected, He asked if I wasn't interested in CPOR, And I explained there was no way I'd be able to attend all the courses on my programme if I were serving in CPOR, He didn't wait another minute, He gave me a blue card, He said I should present it to whoever was in charge after I'd finished the physical, I conclude. My father made a face, clearly displeased. I know I shouldn't have gone to him without telling you, Father, I admit it, but it's done now. The card's in that folder, he asks, looking at the plastic folder on the sideboard. It's in my wallet, I reply. I want to see it, he said. I take my wallet from my trouser pocket, open it, take out the card, hand it to him, he examines it suspiciously, I wait for his reaction. This isn't Damásio's signature, he says, holding up at eye level the sky-blue piece of thick paper shaped like a visiting card with a handwritten code on it and a stamp in rather faint red ink, a stamp I hadn't been able to decipher even after getting home and analysing it carefully, and a swirly signature with a central line crossing from left to right. I have no idea whose it is, I say. Did you tell him which faculty you're in, he asks. Yes, I had to tell him, I reply. And how did he react, my father asks, knowing that being a major in the army involves making decisions that must, to a greater or lesser degree, affect the political life and the freedoms of the people in Porto Alegre, in Rio Grande do Sul, across the whole country, and that his friend Damásio walks in lockstep with his fellow officers in the Armed Forces who aren't too keen on Social Sciences students. He said it was good to see that Célia and Ênio's son was already an adult and knew what he wanted out of life, I say. What else happened, my father asks. Nothing else important, I reply. Without dispelling the expression of total displeasure on his face, he hands the card back to me, picks up the second half of his cracker, brings it to his mouth. Thank you, Dad, Thank you for not tearing up the card or telling me to give it back, I know I did wrong by not telling you I was going to see your friend, I admit. Does your brother know about that card, he asks. I haven't told him, I reply. Look, I don't like what you did, kid, That's the last thing I'm going to say on the matter, and he stands up, gets his jacket, puts it on, takes the mug and plate to the kitchen, washes them, dries them, puts them back in the cupboard, comes back in with his Charles Bronson in *Death Wish II* expression somewhat dampened, puts his hand on my shoulder, says don't tell Lourenço about the card and tells me that, when the time comes for my brother to serve, and if he, my brother, doesn't want to serve, that I'm to offer to help him to get exempted from service, but that I would have to use my skills as a master strategist to manipulate the system to find a way of getting my brother off, that I was forbidden to go see Damásio again, that if I went to Damásio or any other army friend of his then we'd be having words. I say I know what I'm doing. He picks up his holdall, looks like he hasn't heard what I just said, goes out to the hallway that leads to the staircase that takes you to the spacious two-car garage, the garage of his middle-class house, upper-middle-class by Partenon standards, possibly the biggest and best kept house on the street, on the street where our family is the only black family, a street out of keeping with hundreds of other streets in Partenon, where the proportion of black to white families is the reverse. Tense at the suspicion that I'm only one tiny part of his worries, of his war, I stay at the table watching my father move away, he who has always been so clear to me and to my brother that he sees himself as a man who is neither better nor worse than other men, carrying with him his rage and his intention not to make mistakes, never to make a single mistake.

Has Roberta fallen asleep, I asked, looking in the rear-view mirror at the back seat. She has, Lourenço replied, she was up really late writing about her experience in detention, she said she's going to try to send it to some magazine or newspaper, he said. That girl doesn't back down, I said, just imagining all the other new and surprising experiences she would be bringing us. I reckon we're going to have a journalist in the family, he said. I nodded, and then I told him what had happened on that morning in nineteen eighty-four at the Partenon Osório Regiment. Lourenço listened seriously to my account, then said that everything finally made sense, as he'd never seen me so out of control in my life as he had that time in front of the Leopoldina Juvenil. I gave it a few minutes and told him that, despite all my outrage at that idiot sergeant and also at myself for not having done anything while he humiliated the twelve black kids, I still ended up giving the lieutenant the card that Damásio, our father's army friend, had given me to exempt me from service, and I revealed that handing over the card had made me feel, after I got back home and went to my room, like a real piece of shit. He thought that was funny and said there was one thing I wasn't, really I seriously wasn't, and that's a piece of shit, he reclined the passenger seat, said he was going to nap for a bit, he said Anísio would be pleased to see us again, that he hoped Roberta would get along with his daughters, and he straightened his sunglasses on his face, turned down the air conditioning a little, gave me a wake me up if you need anything, big bro, folded his arms and left me to drive his van, at sixty kilometres an hour, which was the speed limit when you were crossing the Taim Ecological Station, squeezed between Lagoon Mirim and the Atlantic Ocean, getting the gusts of the Minuano wind head on, towards Santa Vitória do Palmar and then on towards the Uruguayan border.

ACKNOWLEDGEMENTS

I am grateful for the readings by Danichi Hausen Mizoguchi, Daniele John, Emílio Domingos, Jeferson Tenório, Luíz Heron da Silva, Nicole Witt and her team in Frankfurt, Paula Goldmeier, Paulo Leivas and Stefan Tobler. My particular gratitude to my editor Marcelo Ferroni and his team. I think it's important to say I wouldn't have finished this book without the unconditional support of Morgana Kretzmann, who has been the first reader of almost all the prose I've written in recent years, and the support of my parents, Marlene and Elói, and my brother André. It is right and necessary to acknowledge that the federal judge mentioned by the protagonist in the third chapter of the book is the remarkable gaúcho magistrate Roger Raupp Rios. To readers who aren't from Porto Alegre, I should explain that Partenon is a neighbourhood occupied, for the most part, by black people, it is the place where I grew up, where I lived until I was twenty-two and which – in spite of my having lived in other neighbourhoods in that city, in other cities in Brazil and abroad – in many ways, I have never left. The story told here is a piece of fiction; the characters who take part in it are no more than invented profiles, the scenarios and events configured and reconfigured within it merely fictional.

PHENOTYPES IN PARTICULAR

A Translator's Afterword

Phenotypes was originally written in Portuguese. What you've just read – if you've just read it – is my translation from the Portuguese into English. The original novel, which went by a different title, is the work of Paulo Scott; this translation is the work of Paulo, then me, then our editor, copy-editor and proofreader, who between us found our way to this final version you have in your hands. But I'd like to talk a little about where it started, before I ever got my grubby English fingerprints all over it. That is: Portuguese.

Portuguese – the first language of about 250 million people around the world – is probably the language I translate from the most, so I like to think I know my way around it pretty well, at least as a reader. If I'd wanted to be more accurate, though, I should really have said *Phenotypes* is a translation not simply *from Portuguese* but *from Brazilian Portuguese*. Not that the variations are vast, but there are vocabulary, idiom and syntax variations (the UK/US English split is a reasonable equivalent in some respects); and of course there's a large cultural chasm between the two countries in which these languages live. As it happens, though, this time I'm in luck. My own Portuguese, such as it is (and it so often isn't) is actually Brazilian Portuguese. I have a Brazilian mother, and my understanding of the language comes from more or less annual trips since childhood to be with Brazilian family. When compelled to speak Portuguese, what comes out of my mouth is unmistakably the Brazilian variant. Of all the Portugueses, Brazilian is the one that's deep in my bones, the one whose nuances of tone I catch most readily, unthinking. Paulo's novel, which I presumed to translate, was written in Brazilian Portuguese.

The language gap between two places and the cultural gap are often related, and so it often is between the worlds of Portuguese Portuguese and Brazilian Portuguese. For the purposes of this novel, Brazil's cultural-linguistic particularity is especially striking when talking about race, and when talking about *talking about* race. That conversation is central to the book, and was something over which as a translator – and not least as a white translator – I knew I needed to take the greatest care.

Different countries – and communities within countries – use language differently, because language is shaped by many things, including history and power relations. The parts of a person's identity that may be subject to discrimination, that might occasion derogatory language, that are likely to be weaponised against them, will also be different depending on precisely where in the world you are. Which means that the way race is talked about (and the mixing of races especially) is different in Brazil, a country with a very particular 'rainbow nation' myth of racial harmony, to Portugal. And even more different – this is where it becomes the translator's problem – to the English of the US or the UK, say, whose own delusions of equality rest on quite different histories.

And because cultures don't map exactly onto one another, even when it *looks* like you might be able to map one culture's terminology onto another, you can't. (And what causes offence is not the same everywhere, of course.) The tonal valence of a word like 'mulatto' has good historical reasons for being quite different in Brazil or Portugal, and, for example, the US. One fellow translator suggested I might preserve the cultural particularity by simply retaining all the Brazilian Portuguese terms for skin colour in this English translation, but it was immediately obvious that the totally common Portuguese word 'negro', for the colour black, would generate a lot of interference for the reader given that it is indistinguishable on the page from an English word whose associations and usage are altogether different. You see the problem.

That word, 'negro', is one of the two most common words you might encounter in Brazilian Portuguese (and this book) for the colour black. If you wanted an easy distinction, when referring to people you might think of 'preto' for colour and 'negro' for race and culture, with the latter being commonly used among activist groups, for instance – think of the way we use 'black' and 'Black', perhaps. But that easy distinction, and those English equivalents, are only approximate, and frustratingly inadequate; how those words are used, and the degrees of offence they can sometimes carry, really has no direct and all-purpose English equivalent, and varies depending on who is speaking them. (I'm grateful to Paulo and other friends who helped me understand nuances in the Portuguese usages I hadn't grasped before.) The words used in race and ethnicity discourse in Brazil are different to anywhere in the English-speaking world because that discourse itself, and the history that generated it, is different – translating, then, involves a thoughtful, delicate negotiation of these differences, demanding that a translator be mindful of this conversation and the activism around these words, in their Brazilian context particularly. Language, after all, is never context-less.

But getting a grip on that ever-crucial context gets trickier yet. Brazil is a country of some 210 million people, covering 3.3 million square miles. It is *big*. My own private Brazil is Rio de Janeiro. Paulo tends to write about his birthplace, the southern city of Porto Alegre, which in Brazilian terms is pretty close to Rio but is still nearly a thousand miles away. And that's where my luck runs out, because it's the capital city of a state where I've never even been. So yes, the language of *Phenotypes* is Brazilian Portuguese, but it's more particular than that. An awful lot can happen to a language in a thousand miles. And – again – the gap in culture is wider still. There is so much I don't know. (Even the example I gave above, of the relative uses of 'preto' and 'negro', varies considerably depending on where you are in the country, and who.)

To translate this book, then, knowing my Brazilian Portuguese was not nearly enough. It required acquiring – or occasionally faking – knowledge about a local world I didn't know at all. Along the way, I've needed to learn about foods specific only to this southern region, to understand the workings of this particular state's criminal justice system, and to spend more time than you can imagine on Google Maps trying to work out how certain Porto Alegre streets meet certain other Porto Alegre streets, and what can be seen from where, and how big the barracks door might be. I needed to know everything about everything, in order to be able to name it, again, for you.

Not *explain* it, mind – just name it. I'm not too bothered about the explaining. A translator, like any writer, must decide what sort of allowances should be made to their reader, how much hand-holding they should get to help them navigate the book's culture. If you're reading this note after having read the translation, you'll have gathered that my final answer was 'not much' – this translation is not in the business of explaining a lot, nor indeed of making loads of stylistic concessions. Remember, most local cultural references will be every bit as mysterious to the great majority of Portuguese speakers too, just as a book set in a specific community in New Orleans will be full of things that could baffle a reader in Inverness and vice versa, a common language dividing them notwithstanding. So if an English-language reader doesn't get the significance of every reference, I'm entirely comfortable with that. (I should here acknowledge the efforts of this book's brilliant editor, Jeremy Davies, who I suspect wanted me to be kinder to you in this respect. Anything you found inexplicable in your reading is my fault alone.)

I should say, of course, that even just naming things in a language to which they aren't native is seldom easy. Even having understood (well, OK, *sort of* understood) the criminal justice system in Rio Grande do Sul, it still doesn't map directly – noun for noun, procedure for procedure, role for role, institution for institution – onto the English-language criminal justice system. And besides, there's obviously no such thing as a global 'English-language criminal justice system' equally familiar to all. Because I don't know whether you, our new reader, are in York or New York, in Dublin or Durban. You might, for that matter, be an English speaker in Porto Alegre who understands this whole local legal structure already. (In which case I can't help feeling you ought to have made yourself known earlier. I could have used your help.)

So we have a book written in Big-Global-Language Portuguese, but more specifically Brazilian Portuguese, but more specifically still from Porto Alegre (apart from the odd scene in the nation's distant capital). And each of these narrowings of focus changes the world of the book, and what every little cultural signal implies, and how that world gets articulated in words.

But it gets worse! The novel's home state of Rio Grande do Sul has a population of about twelve million people. And my novelist, brilliant though he is, is only one of them. So the novel was written in the Porto Alegre Brazilian Portuguese *of Paulo Scott*. Because each one of us, whether we are writers or not, has what linguists call an idiolect – that is, a use of language that's unique to the individual – and that thing, that tiny and very particular thing, is *really* what I'm dealing with here.

In its past life, the novel's title was *Marrom e amarelo*, which means 'Brown and yellow' and refers to the skin colour of two of the characters. Both of those adjectives are used in the English-speaking world as racial descriptors – in my UK, the first might suggest a person from South Asia or of South Asian heritage; the second is an old racial slur relating to East Asia. The Brazilian title intends neither of these – the words are references to the narrator and his brother, sons of a Black family, who are mixed-race but who present quite differently, one dark-skinned and the other light. 'Brown' and 'Yellow' are simply their respective nicknames. This is not common usage in Portuguese; it's not Brazilian-Portuguese; it's not even Porto-Alegre-Brazilian-Portuguese. It is, however, what the author's own father really calls him and his brother. It's the language of one family. If you walked two houses up the street from them, or two houses down, you'd find words used differently. It's a vast global language at its most granular. This book is written in the language of Paulo Scott.

In part, the language of Paulo Scott is mercifully familiar to me – for one thing, I've translated him before, which always helps. Last time we worked together (on *Nowhere People*, back in 2014), I wrote an essay about the experience for *Asymptote*, in which I described the challenges of attending to this writer's linguistic particularity, creating sentences to match the author's own, preserving all the stylistic and lexical idiosyncrasies that I loved as a reader but which gave me sleepless nights when it came to making an English text do the same. But the more aware I am that the language and its effect are utterly contingent upon their particular origin and sometimes granular-level context, the more preposterous seems the very idea of recreating the whole thing in an altogether different cultural system – and a language that isn't even Portuguese at all! So what is my role, exactly?

A recent Goodreads review of one of my books expressed a kind of generalised suspicion about the trustworthiness of translation in general, before grudgingly concluding that the one in question probably was 'honest'. Which I found a fascinating word for what it revealed about the reader's general misgivings about the whole translating enterprise – but there's also something in it, isn't there? I wouldn't use the word 'honest' myself, but certainly we want to produce a representation of the original book that is – what – maybe *truthful*? A truthful depiction of the book and its world. This means, for me, not adapting it to the expectations or the sensibilities of its new readers; it means resisting occasionally tempting changes to the author's style (when discussing the edits with Jeremy, I tried to draw a distinction between clarification of the style, which I'm keen on, and simplification, which I'm not); and it means not smoothing out the characters and their world to suit somebody else's taboos, however squeamish this truthful representation might make me.

Marrom e amarelo – this book's first incarnation – is a book of great literary sophistication; but it's also a significant and thoughtful and sometimes challenging contribution to its country's conversations about race. (It was also launched into a publishing world that is itself – like ours – still hugely imbalanced in favour of the white population.) Among other things, Paulo's book highlights the inadequacies – or even sometimes dangers – of seeing precise racial identification as being subject to a single uncomplicated metric. This translated version of the novel does not 'adapt' the original to suit its possible readers (nor could it do that with any honesty); it doesn't pretend that racial discourses are the same everywhere, that they map tidily onto one another – in language or lived experience – nor that the same things are likely to cause offence. Rather it represents as best it can one experience's specificities, and works on an assumption that our sometimes

dogmatic attitudes to singular, simplified, acceptable discourses are in fact culturally and historically contingent, and
that mine – or yours – might even benefit from a challenge
by other realities elsewhere, the more individual, the more
personal, the more particular the better. Ideally, translation
should do this always, I think.

DANIEL HAHN
Lewes, August 2021

Dear readers,

As well as relying on bookshop sales, And Other Stories relies on subscriptions from people like you for many of our books, whose stories other publishers often consider too risky to take on.

Our subscribers don't just make the books physically happen. They also help us approach booksellers, because we can demonstrate that our books already have readers and fans. And they give us the security to publish in line with our values, which are collaborative, imaginative and 'shamelessly literary'.

All of our subscribers:

- receive a first-edition copy of each of the books they subscribe to
- are thanked by name at the end of our subscriber-supported books
- receive little extras from us by way of thank you, for example: postcards created by our authors

BECOME A SUBSCRIBER,
OR GIVE A SUBSCRIPTION TO A FRIEND

Visit andotherstories.org/subscriptions to help make our books happen. You can subscribe to books we're in the process of making. To purchase books we have already published, we urge you to support your local or favourite bookshop and order directly from them – the often unsung heroes of publishing.

OTHER WAYS TO GET INVOLVED

If you'd like to know about upcoming events and reading groups (our foreign-language reading groups help us choose books to publish, for example) you can:

- join our mailing list at: andotherstories.org
- follow us on Twitter: @andothertweets
- join us on Facebook: facebook.com/AndOtherStoriesBooks
- admire our books on Instagram: @andotherpics
- follow our blog: andotherstories.org/ampersand

THIS BOOK WAS MADE POSSIBLE
THANKS TO THE SUPPORT OF

A Cudmore
Aaron McEnery
Aaron Schneider
Abigail Howell
Abigail Walton
Adam Clarke
Adam Lenson
Adrian Astur Alvarez
Aifric Campbell
Aisha McLean
Ajay Sharma
Alan Donnelly
Alan Felsenthal
Alastair Gillespie
Alastair Whitson
Albert Puente
Alex Pearce
Alex Ramsey
Alexander Williams
Alexandra Stewart
Alexandra Stewart
Alexandra Tammaro
Alexandra Tilden
Alexandra Webb
Ali Riley
Ali Smith
Ali Usman
Alice Morgan
Alice Smith
Alice Toulmin
Alice Wilkinson
Alison Hardy
Alison Winston
Aliya Rashid
Alyssa Rinaldi
Alyssa Tauber
Amado Floresca

Amaia Gabantxo
Amalia Gladhart
Amanda Astley
Amanda Dalton
Amanda Geenen
Amanda Read
Amanda
Amber Da
Amitav Hajra
Amy Bessent
Amy Bojang
Amy Finch
Amy Janiczek
Amy Tabb
Ana Novak
Anastasia Carver
Andra Dusu
Andrea Barlien
Andrea Brownstone
Andrea Oyarzabal
  Koppes
Andrea Reece
Andrew Kerr-Jarrett
Andrew Marston
Andrew McCallum
Andrew Ratomski
Andrew Rego
Andy Corsham
Andy Marshall
Andy Turner
Angelica Ribichini
Angus Walker
Anita Starosta
Ann Rees
Anna-Maria Aurich
Anna French
Anna Gibson

Anna Hawthorne
Anna Milsom
Anna Zaranko
Anne Carus
Anne Boileau Clarke
Anne Craven
Anne Edyvean
Anne Kangley
Anne O' Brien
Anne Sticksel
Anne Withane
Anonymous
Anonymous
Anthony Alexander
Anthony Cotton
Anthony Quinn
Antonia Lloyd-Jones
Antonia Saske
Antony Pearce
Aoife Boyd
Arabella Bosworth
Archie Davies
Aron Negyesi
Aron Trauring
Arthur John Rowles
Asako Serizawa
Ashleigh Sutton
Audrey Mash
Audrey Small
Barbara Bettsworth
Barbara Mellor
Barbara Robinson
Barbara Spicer
Barry John Fletcher
Barry Norton
Bea Karol Burks
Becky Cherriman

Becky Matthewson
Ben Buchwald
Ben Schofield
Ben Thornton
Ben Walter
Benjamin Judge
Benjamin Pester
Beth Heim de Bera
Bethan Kent
Beverley Thomas
Bianca Duec
Bianca Jackson
Bianca Winter
Bill Fletcher
Björn Warren
Bjørnar Djupevik Hagen
Blazej Jedras
Briallen Hopper
Brian Anderson
Brian Byrne
Brian Conn
Brian Smith
Brigita Ptackova
Briony Hey
Buck Johnston
Burkhard Fehsenfeld
Caitlin Halpern
Caitriona Lally
Cam Scott
Cameron Adams
Cameron Lindo
Camilla Imperiali
Campbell McEwan
Carla Ballin
Carla Castanos
Carole Parkhouse
Carolina Pineiro
Caroline West
Catharine Braithwaite
Catherine Barton
Catherine Lambert

Catherine Tandy
Catherine Williamson
Cathryn Siegal-
  Bergman
Cathy Galvin
Cathy Sowell
Catie Kosinski
Catrine Bollerslev
Catriona Gibbs
Cecilia Rossi
Cecilia Uribe
Chantal Lyons
Chantal Wright
Charlene Huggins
Charles Fernyhough
Charles Kovach
Charles Dee Mitchell
Charles Rowe
Charlie Levin
Charlie Small
Charlotte Bruton
Charlotte Coulthard
Charlotte Middleton
Charlotte Whittle
China Miéville
Chloe Baird
Chris Blackmore
Chris Gostick
Chris Gribble
Chris Holmes
Chris Johnstone
Chris Lintott
Chris McCann
Chris Potts
Chris Stergalas
Chris Stevenson
Chris Thornton
Christian Schuhmann
Christina Moutsou
Christine Bartels
Christine Elliott

Christopher Allen
Christopher Homfray
Christopher Smith
Christopher Stout
Ciara Ní Riain
Ciarán Schütte
Claire Adams
Claire Brooksby
Claire Mackintosh
Claire Morrison
Claire Smith
Claire Williams
Clare Young
Clarice Borges
Claudia Mazzoncini
Cliona Quigley
Colin Denyer
Colin Hewlett
Colin Matthews
Collin Brooke
Cornelia Svedman
Cortina Butler
Courtney Lilly
Craig Kennedy
Cynthia De La Torre
Cyrus Massoudi
Daisy Savage
Dale Wisely
Dan Martin
Daniel Coxon
Daniel Gillespie
Daniel Hahn
Daniel Hester-Smith
Daniel Jones
Daniel Oudshoorn
Daniel Sanford
Daniel Stewart
Daniel Syrovy
Daniela Steierberg
Darren Davies
Darryll Rogers

Dave Lander
David Anderson
David Cowan
David Davies
David Gould
David Greenlaw
David Hebblethwaite
David Higgins
David Johnson-Davies
David Leverington
David F Long
David McIntyre
David Miller
David and Lydia Pell
David Richardson
David Shriver
David Smith
David Thornton
Davis MacMillan
Dawn Bass
Dean Taucher
Deb Hughes
Debbie Pinfold
Deborah Herron
Declan Gardner
Declan O'Driscoll
Deirdre Nic Mhathuna
Denis Larose
Denis Stillewagt &
 Anca Fronescu
Denise Bretländer
Denton Djurasevich
Desiree Mason
Diana Baker Smith
Diane Salisbury
Dietrich Menzel
Dina Abdul-Wahab
Dinesh Prasad
Dominic Nolan
Dominick Santa
 Cattarina

Dominique Hudson
Doug Wallace
Duncan Clubb
Duncan Macgregor
Duncan Marks
Dustin Haviv
Dyanne Prinsen
Earl James
Ebba Tornérhielm
Ed Tronick
Ekaterina Beliakova
Elaine Frances
Elaine Juzl
Eleanor Maier
Eleanor Updegraff
Elena Esparza
Elif Aganoglu
Elina Zicmane
Elisabeth Cook
Elizabeth Braswell
Elizabeth Coombes
Elizabeth Draper
Elizabeth Franz
Elizabeth Guss
Elizabeth Leach
Elizabeth Seals
Elizabeth Wood
Ellen Beardsworth
Emily Armitage
Emily Dixon
Emily Jang
Emily Webber
Emma Barraclough
Emma Bielecki
Emma Louise Grove
Emma Morgan
Emma Post
Eric Anderson
Erin Cameron Allen
Esméc de Heer
Esther Donnelly

Esther Kinsky
Ethan Madarieta
Ethan White
Eva Mitchell
Ewan Tant
F Gary Knapp
Felicity Williams
Felix Valdivieso
Finbarr Farragher
Fiona Liddle
Fiona Mozley
Forrest Pelsue
Fran Sanderson
Frances Christodoulou
Frances Thiessen
Francesca Brooks
Francesca Hemery
Francesca Rhydderch
Francis Mathias
Frank Rodrigues
Frank van Orsouw
Frankie Mullin
Frauke Matthes
Freddie Radford
Friederike Knabe
Gala Copley
Garan Holcombe
Gavin Aitchison
Gavin Smith
Gawain Espley
Gemma Bird
Gemma Doyle
Genaro Palomo Jr
Geoff Thrower
Geoffrey Cohen
Geoffrey Urland
George Stanbury
Georgia Shomidie
Georgina Hildick-
 Smith
Georgina Norton

Gerry Craddock
Gill Boag-Munroe
Gillian Grant
Gina Heathcote
Glenn Russell
Gordon Cameron
Gosia Pennar
Graham Blenkinsop
Graham R Foster
Graham Page
Grant Rintoul
Gregory Philp
Hadil Balzan
Halina Schiffman-
  Shilo
Hamish Russell
Hannah Bucknell
Hannah Freeman
Hannah Jane
  Lownsbrough
Hannah Morris
Hannah Procter
Hannah Rapley
Hannah Vidmark
Hanora Bagnell
Hans Lazda
Harriet Stiles
Haydon Spenceley
Hayley Cox
Hazel Smoczynska
Heidi Gilhooly
Helen Moor
Helena Buffery
Henriette Magerstaedt
Henrike Laehnemann
Henry Patino
Holly Down
Howard Robinson
Hyoung-Won Park
Iain Forsyth
Ian Hagues

Ian McMillan
Ian Mond
Ian Whiteley
Ida Grochowska
Ifer Moore
Ines Alfano
Ingunn Vallumroed
Iona Stevens
Irene Croal
Irene Mansfield
Irina Tzanova
Isabella Garment
Isabella Weibrecht
Isabelle Schneider
Isobel Foxford
Ivy Lin
J Drew Hancock-Teed
Jacinta Perez Gavilan
  Torres
Jack Brown
Jacqueline Lademann
Jacqui Jackson
Jade Yiu
Jake Baldwinson
James Beck
James Crossley
James Cubbon
James Elkins
James Greer
James Kinsley
James Lee
James Lehmann
James Leonard
James Lesniak
James Leveque
James Mewis
James Portlock
James Scudamore
Jamie Cox
Jamie Mollart
Jan Hicks

Jan Leah Lowe
Jane Bryce
Jane Dolman
Jane Fairweather
Jane Leuchter
Jane Roberts
Jane Roberts
Jane Willborn
Jane Woollard
Janelle Ward
Janis Carpenter
Jasmine Gideon
Jason Lever
Jason Montano
Jason Sim
Jason Timermanis
Jason Whalley
Jayne Watson
JE Crispin
Jeanne Guyon
Jeff Collins
Jen Hardwicke
Jenifer Logie
Jennifer Arnold
Jennifer Higgins
Jennifer Mills
Jennifer Watts
Jenny Huth
Jenny Newton
Jeremy Koenig
Jeremy Morton
Jerry Simcock
Jess Hazlewood
Jess Wilder
Jess Wood
Jesse Coleman
Jesse Hara
Jessica Gately
Jessica Mello
Jessica Queree
Jessica Weetch

Jethro Soutar
Jill Harrison
Jo Keyes
Joanna Luloff
Joao Pedro Bragatti
  Winckler
JoDee Brandon
Jodie Adams
Joe Gill
Joe Huggins
Joel Garza
Joel Swerdlow
Johannes Holmqvist
Johannes Menzel
John Bennett
John Berube
John Bogg
John Carnahan
John Conway
John Down
John Gent
John Guyatt
John Hodgson
John Kelly
John Reid
John Royley
John Shaw
John Steigerwald
John Wallace
John Walsh
John Winkelman
Jolene Smith
Jon Riches
Jon Talbot
Jonathan Blaney
Jonathan Fiedler
Jonathan Harris
Jonathan Huston
Jonathan Paterson
Jonathan Ruppin
Joni Chan

Jonny Kiehlmann
Jordana Carlin
José Machado
Joseph Camilleri
Joseph Darlington
Joseph Novak
Joseph Schreiber
Joseph Thomas
Josh Calvo
Josh Sumner
Joshua Davis
Joshua McNamara
Joy Paul
Judith Gruet-Kaye
Judith Hannan
Judy Davies
Julia Sanches
Julia Von Dem
  Knesebeck
Julian Molina
Julie Greenwalt
Juliet Birkbeck
Juliet Swann
Jupiter Jones
Juraj Janik
Justin Anderson
Justine Goodchild
Justine Sherwood
JW Mersky
Kaarina Hollo
Kaelyn Davis
Kaja R Anker-Rasch
Karl Kleinknecht &
  Monika Motylinska
Katarzyna
  Bartoszynska
Kate Attwooll
Kate Beswick
Kate Carlton-Reditt
Kate Morgan
Kate Procter

Kate Shires
Katharine Robbins
Katherine Brabon
Katherine Mackinnon
Kathryn Edwards
Kathryn Hemmann
Kathryn Williams
Katia Wengraf
Katie Brown
Katie Freeman
Katie Grant
Katie Smart
Katy Robinson
Keith Walker
Ken Geniza
Kenneth Blythe
Kenneth Michaels
Kent McKernan
Kerry Parke
Kieran Rollin
Kieron James
Kim White
Kirsten Hey
Kirsty Doole
Kirsty Simpkins
KL Ee
Klara Rešetič
Kris Ann Trimis
Kristen Tcherneshoff
Krystale Tremblay-
  Moll
Krystine Phelps
Kyra Wilder
Lacy Wolfe
Lana Selby
Laura Clarke
Laura Ling
Laura Pugh
Laura Rangeley
Lauren Pout
Laurence Laluyaux

Lee Harbour
Leona Iosifidou
Leonora Randall
Leslie Jacobson
Liliana Lobato
Lily Blacksell
Lily Robert-Foley
Lindsay Attree
Lindsay Brammer
Lindsey Ford
Lindsey Harbour
Lisa Agostini
Lisa Bean
Lisa Dillman
Lisa Leahigh
Lisa Simpson
Lisa Weizenegger
Liz Clifford
Liz Ketch
Lorna Bleach
Lottie Smith
Louise Evans
Louise Greenberg
Louise Jolliffe
Louise Smith
Luc Daley
Luc Verstraete
Lucas J Medeiros
Lucinda Smith
Lucy Gorman
Lucy Leeson-Smith
Lucy Moffatt
Luise von Flotow
Luke Loftiss
Lydia Trethewey
Lynda Graham
Lyndia Thomas
Lynn Fung
Lynn Martin
Lynn Ross
Maeve Lambe

Maggie Humm
Maggie Kerkman
Malgorzata Rokicka
Manu Chastelain
Marcel Inhoff
Marco Medjimorec
Margaret Cushen
Mari-Liis Calloway
Maria Ahnhem Farrar
Maria Hill
Maria Lomunno
Maria Losada
Marie Cloutier
Marie Donnelly
Marijana Rimac
Marina Castledine
Mario Sifuentez
Marja S Laaksonen
Mark Bridgman
Mark Sargent
Mark Scott
Mark Sheets
Mark Sztyber
Mark Walsh
Mark Waters
Marlene Simoes
Martin Brown
Martin Nathan
Martin Eric Rodgers
Mary Angela Brevidoro
Mary Heiss
Mary Wang
Maryse Meijer
Mathias Ruthner
Mathilde Pascal
Matt Davies
Matt Greene
Matt O'Connor
Matthew Adamson
Matthew Black
Matthew Cooke

Matthew Eatough
Matthew Francis
Matthew Gill
Matthew Lowe
Matthew Woodman
Matthias Rosenberg
Maura Cheeks
Maureen Cullen
Max Cairnduff
Max Longman
Max McCabe
Meaghan Delahunt
Meg Lovelock
Megan Holt
Megan Taylor
Megan Wittling
Mel Pryor
Melissa Beck
Melissa Stogsdill
Meredith Martin
Michael Bichko
Michael Boog
Michael Dodd
Michael James
  Eastwood
Michael Floyd
Michael Gavin
Michael Kuhn
Michael Roess
Michael Schneiderman
Michelle Mercaldo
Michelle Perkins
Miguel Head
Mike Turner
Mildred Nicotera
Miles Smith-Morris
Miranda Gold
Misa Sekiguchi
Moira Garland
Molly Foster
Mona Arshi

Morayma Jimenez
Moremi Apata-
  Omisore
Moriah Haefner
Morven Dooner
Muireann Maguire
Myles Nolan
N Tsolak
Nancy Foley
Nancy Jacobson
Nancy Kerkman
Nancy Oakes
Nancy Peters
Nanda Griffioen
Naomi Morauf
Naomi Sparks
Natalia Reyes
Natalie Ricks
Nathalie Atkinson
Nathalie Karagiannis
Nathalie Teitler
Nathan McNamara
Nathan Rowley
Nathan Weida
Nicholas Brown
Nicholas Jowett
Nicholas Rutherford
Nick Chapman
Nick James
Nick Marshall
Nick Nelson & Rachel
  Eley
Nick Sidwell
Nick Twemlow
Nicola Cook
Nicola Hart
Nicola Mira
Nicola Sandiford
Nicola Scott
Nicole Joy
Nicole Matteini

Nicoletta Asciuto
Nigel Fishburn
Niki Sammut
Nina Nickerson
Nina Todorova
Odilia Corneth
Olga Alexandru
Olga Zilberbourg
Pamela Tao
Pankaj Mishra
Pat Winslow
Patricia Aronsson
Patrick Hawley
Patrick Hoare
Patrick McGuinness
Paul Cray
Paul Ewing
Paul Flaig
Paul Jones
Paul Munday
Paul Nightingale
Paul Robinson
Paul Scott
Paul Thompson and
  Gordon McArthur
Pauline Drury
Pavlos Stavropoulos
Penelope Hewett-
  Brown
Perlita Payne
Peter Edwards
Peter Griffin
Peter Halliday
Peter Hayden
Peter McBain
Peter McCambridge
Peter Rowland
Peter Taplin
Peter Van de Maele
  and Narina Dahms
Peter Wells

Petra Stapp
Phil Bartlett
Philip Herbert
Philip Warren
Philip Williams
Philipp Jarke
Phillipa Clements
Phoebe Millerwhite
Phyllis Reeve
Pia Figge
Piet Van Bockstal
Prakash Nayak
Priya Sharma
Rachael de Moravia
Rachael Williams
Rachel Carter
Rachel Matheson
Rachel Meacock
Rachel Van Riel
Ramona Pulsford
Raymond Manzo
Rebecca Braun
Rebecca Carter
Rebecca Ketcherside
Rebecca Moss
Rebecca O'Reilly
Rebecca Parry
Rebecca Peer
Rebecca Roadman
Rebecca Rose
Rebecca Rosenthal
Rebecca Shaak
Rebecca Söregi
Rebekka Bremmer
Renee Thomas
Rhiannon Armstrong
Rich Sutherland
Richard Ellis
Richard Gwyn
Richard Harrison
Richard Mann

Richard Mansell
Richard Priest
Richard Shea
Richard Soundy
Rick Tucker
Riley & Alyssa
  Manning
Rita Kaar
Rita O'Brien
Rob Kidd
Robert Arnott
Robert Gillett
Robert Hamilton
Robert Hannah
Roberto Hull
Robin McLean
Robin Taylor
Roger Newton
Roger Ramsden
Rory Williamson
Rosalind May
Rosalind Ramsay
Rosanna Foster
Rose Crichton
Rose Pearce
Ross MacIntyre
Roxanne O'Del Ablett
Roz Simpson
Rupert Ziziros
Ruth Deyermond
Ruth Field
Ryan Day
S Italiano
Sabine Little
Sally Arkinstall
Sally Baker
Sally Bramley
Sally Ellis
Sally Hemsley
Sally Warner
Sam Gordon

Sam Reese
Sam Southwood
Samantha Pavlov
Samuel Crosby
Samuel Wright
Sara Bea
Sara Kittleson
Sara Sherwood
Sara Warshawski
Sarah Arboleda
Sarah Blunden
Sarah Brewer
Sarah Farley
Sarah Lucas
Sarah Manvel
Sarah Pybus
Sarah Spitz
Sarah Stevns
Scott Astrada
Scott Chiddister
Scott Henkle
Scott Russell
Scott Simpson
Sean Kottke
Sez Kiss
Shane Horgan
Shannon Knapp
Sharon Dogar
Sharon McCammon
Shauna Gilligan
Shauna Rogers
Sheila Duffy
Sian Hannah
Sienna Kang
Simon Clark
Simon Pitney
Simon Robertson
Simone Martelossi
SK Grout
Sophia Wickham
Sophie Church

ST Dabbagh
Stacy Rodgers
Stefanie Schrank
Stefano Mula
Stephan Eggum
Stephanie Lacava
Stephanie Miller
Stephen Cunliffe
Stephen Pearsall
Steve Clough
Steve Dearden
Steve James
Steve Tuffnell
Steven Norton
Stewart Eastham
Stuart Grey
Stuart Phillips
Stuart Wilkinson
Su Bonfanti
Susan Bamford
Susan Clegg
Susan Ferguson
Susan Jaken
Susan Winter
Suzanne Colangelo
  Lillis
Suzanne Kirkham
Sylvie Zannier-Betts
Tamara Larsen
Tamsin Walker
Tania Hershman
Tara Roman
Tasmin Maitland
Taylor Ffitch
Teresa Werner
Tess Lewis
Tess McAlister
The Mighty Douche
  Softball Team
Thom Cuell
Thom Keep

Thomas Campbell
Thomas Fritz
Thomas Mitchell
Thomas Smith
Thomas van den Bout
Tian Zheng
Tiffany Lehr
Tim Kelly
Tim Schneider
Tim Scott
Timothy Cummins
Tina Rotherham-
  Winqvist
Toby Halsey
Toby Ryan
Tom Darby
Tom Doyle
Tom Franklin
Tom Gray
Tom Stafford
Tom Whatmore

Tory Jeffay
Tracy Bauld
Tracy Heuring
Tracy Lee-Newman
Tracy Shapley
Trevor Wald
Tricia Durdey
Tricia Pillay
Ursula Dawson
Valerie O'Riordan
Vanessa Baird
Vanessa Dodd
Vanessa Fernandez
  Greene
Vanessa Fuller
Vanessa Heggie
Vanessa Nolan
Vanessa Rush
Victor Meadowcroft
Victoria Eld
Victoria Goodbody

Victoria Huggins
Victoria Larroque
Vijay Pattisapu
Wendy Langridge
William Black
William
  Brockenborough
William Dennehy
William Franklin
William Richard
William Schwaber
William Sitters
William Wood
Yoora Yi Tenen
Zachary Maricondia
Zachary Whyte
Zara Rahman
Zareena Amiruddin
Zoe Taylor
Zoe Thomas
Zoë Brasier

NOWHERE PEOPLE

PAULO SCOTT
TRANSLATED BY DANIEL HAHN

Nowhere People

Translated by Daniel Hahn

WINNER OF THE MACHADO DE ASSIS PRIZE

Driving home, law student Paulo passes a figure at the side of the road. The indigenous girl stands in the heavy rain, as if waiting for something. Paulo gives her a lift to her family's roadside camp.

Through sudden shifts in the characters' lives, this novel takes in the whole story: telling of love, loss and family, it spans the worlds of São Paulo's rich kids and dispossessed Guarani Indians along Brazil's highways. One man escapes into an immigrant squatter's life in London, while another's performance activism leads to unexpected fame on YouTube.

Written from the gut, *Nowhere People* is a raw and passionate classic in the making about our need for a home.

.　　.　　.

'Of all the novels of the last five years, I really love *Nowhere People*. It is one hell of a book. And amazing in its structure.'
João Gilberto Noll

'One of Scott's many merits is the audacity he shows, on many levels. Scott dares to create one of the most interesting voices in recent fiction. And that is the voice of a Guarani Indian girl. Maína is far from the stereotypes of the "noble savage" that orientate our literature and culture. Maína speaks.'
O Globo

'Immensely powerful. [...] This novel tackles post-dictatorship Brazilian ideologies better than anything else in fiction.'
O Estado de São Paulo

'*Nowhere People* is an inexhaustible font of surprises that the author's firm hand manages to harmonise.'
Rascunho

CURRENT & UPCOMING BOOKS

PAULO SCOTT was born in 1966 in Porto Alegre, in southern Brazil, and grew up in a working-class neighbourhood. At university, he was an active member of the student political movement and was also involved in Brazil's re-democratisation process. For fourteen years he taught law at university. He has now published six books of fiction and seven of poetry, as well as one graphic novel. He has lived in London, Rio de Janeiro and Garopaba, and moved to São Paulo in 2019 to focus on writing full-time.

DANIEL HAHN is a writer, editor and translator with around eighty books to his name. His work has won the Independent Foreign Fiction Prize, the Blue Peter Book Award and the International Dublin Literary Award, and been shortlisted for the Man Booker International Prize, among others.